EVERYBODY'S DARLING

A Novel

Jayne M. Wesler

This is a work of fiction. Names, characters, places, and incidents either are the product of the author's imagination or are used fictitiously, and any resemblance to actual persons, living or dead, businesses, companies, events, or locales is entirely coincidental.

First Printing: January 28, 2023

Milford, PA

Saint Cloud, FL

ISBN 979-8-9864124-1-2

Library of Congress 2022917358

Published by Jayne Wesler Group LLC

JayneWesler.com

Jayne M. Wesler is an author, coach, speaker, licensed clinical social worker, and attorney. She is the author of Handbook for Parents of Children with Special Needs: *A Therapeutic and Legal Approach; Hurts So Good: An Orgasm of Tears; Hurts So Good: An Orgasm of Tears Workbook; No Bones About It: Increase Your Bone Density Without Medication; the novel Railroaded, Reverse Osteoporosis & Osteopenia Without Medication: Evidence-Based Interventions, and Feed Your Bones! A Nutritional Workbook for Increased Bone Density & Bone Strength*. Ms. Wesler, a partner in the law firm of Sussan, Greenwald, & Wesler, has for decades helped students with disabilities obtain the kind of educational programming that helps them achieve success.

As a psychotherapist, Ms. Wesler has worked with adults, teens, and children in various settings, including both inpatient and outpatient, individual and group therapy. As a member of multiple Child Study Teams, Ms. Wesler conducted evaluations, wrote IEPs, case managed elementary-school students, high-school students, and students placed in specialized, private-school programs. She also developed and facilitated various psychotherapy groups.

Ms. Wesler enjoys spending time with family and friends, hiking, skiing, scuba diving, snorkeling, working out, reading, traveling, and cooking.

Other books by Jayne Wesler

RAILROADED:

A NOVEL

Eighteen-year-old Will Van Dalen finds himself betrayed and framed for a crime he didn't commit. Backed into a corner, struggling with attention-deficit disorder, and surrounded by a rash of recent suicides, is he desperate enough to make a permanent escape?

Will a brother's love transcend blood and betrayal?

Lawyer Liz Myler fights for truth, justice, and the magic that changes the course of human life. But can she save Will?

Open this book to find the answers…

Available on Amazon.com

Barnesandnoble.com

Discoverbooks.com

Abebooks.com

Alibris.com

Walmart.com

Thriftbooks.com

REVERSE OSTEOPOROSIS AND OSTEOPENIA WITHOUT MEDICATION: EVIDENCE-BASED INTERVENTIONS

You've been diagnosed with osteopenia or osteoporosis. Now what? Have you been told to take medication? Do you know the risks and discomfort of those medications? Do you know that approximately 80% of patients are unable to stay on the medications for the recommended amount of time, thus erasing the alleged benefits? Are you aware that medication offers no significant protection against fracture? Are you aware that DEXA scans cannot predict a fracture? Did your health care provider advise you that other options exist? Author and professional problem-solver (psychotherapist, attorney, coach) Jayne M Wesler has personally grappled with the challenge of osteoporosis and the looming threat of medication. She chose natural interventions that successfully increased her own bone density without medication.

FEED YOUR BONES!:
A Nutritional Workbook for Increased Bone Density & Bone Strength

In this detailed yet simple workbook, Jayne Wesler wrestles with the question of which diet best promotes good bone health. After years of reading and researching this topic, Ms. Wesler outlines a plan you can follow, one about which you can be certain.

Jayne Wesler was diagnosed with osteoporosis at the relatively young age of 50. Over the next four years, her condition worsened, yet her physicians did not advise her of the many interventions she could use to improve her bone health. Left to her own devices, she investigated. After a year of trial and error, much anguish, and a great deal of hard work, she was successful!

Compelled to continue to help herself and the millions of women and men who suffer from osteopenia and osteoporosis, Ms. Wesler developed a program to improve bone health. This led to the publication of three books on bone health, the development of a webinar, and a four-week course designed to help those at risk of OP develop and adhere to their own individualized bone-building plans. While developing the four-week course, Ms. Wesler returned, once again, to the question: Am I really eating right for my bone health?

If you, too, ask this question, open this workbook, and find the answers within. In this detailed yet simple workbook, Jayne Wesler wrestles with the question of which diet best promotes good bone health. After years of reading and researching this topic, Ms. Wesler outlines a plan you can follow, one about which you can be certain.

NO BONES ABOUT IT:

HOW TO INCREASE YOUR BONE DENSITY WITHOUT MEDICATION

The purpose of this book is to reach the millions of women and men who are diagnosed with bone loss and to give them—and maybe you, dear reader—a viable alternative to taking medication to increase their bone density.

Have you gotten a diagnosis of osteopenia or osteoporosis? Has someone you love been diagnosed? If you're freaking out and wondering what you can do, take a deep breath. **There are steps you can take to strengthen your bones**. This diagnosis does not define your life. Open this book and keep reading to learn how you can assess your risk factors, summon and utilize your resources, and make positive changes in the health of your bones.

Available on Amazon.com

Walmart.com

BarnesandNoble.com

The HANDBOOK FOR PARENTS OF CHILDREN WITH SPECIAL NEEDS: A THERAPEUTIC AND LEGAL APPROACH

As a lawyer, psychotherapist, and former Child Study Team member who practiced exclusively on behalf of children with special needs, Jayne Wesler has helped hundreds, if not thousands, of parents obtain educational programs that led to their child's success. In this book, she shares information with you from federal and state law, federal and state regulations, psychotherapeutic techniques, and her experience so that you, too, can change the trajectory of your child's life. If you use the techniques, tools, and knowledge she provides to you, you can and will obtain successful programs for your child to help them succeed in school—the sooner, the better.

Children grow so quickly that when they need help, they need it *now*. Don't wait. Do it today. You'll be glad you did.

"This book is an easy-to-read, go-to manual containing pearls of wisdom and accessible references for creating your child's educational blueprint. Jayne Wesler created this handbook blending both wisdom and heart!"

Jill Brooks, PhD, clinical neuropsychologist, Head 2 Head Consulting

"With her background as a psychotherapist and an education attorney, Jayne Wesler has written a thoughtful and practical guide for parents of children with special needs looking to navigate the sometimes turbulent and confusing waters of the special education world."

Daniel DaSilva, PhD, pediatric neuropsychologist, Morris Psychological Group

"This is an essential guide for parents seeking the best education for their children, important information from an expert attorney, educator, and psychotherapist. A must-read."

Ellen Fenster-Kuehl, PhD, licensed psychologist

"The book you hold in your hand is a blueprint to navigating the complexities of educational programming. Attorney and psychotherapist Jayne Wesler integrates her knowledge and offers a unique perspective on how to truly transform your child's life."

Melissa Fiorito-Grafman, PhD, clinical neuropsychologist, Center for Neuropsychology & Psychotherapy

"Attorney and psychotherapist Jayne Wesler shares her practical knowledge on how to truly transform your child's life."

Dana Henning, EdD, Education Consultant, Dana Henning Training Programs

HURTS SO GOOD: AN ORGASM OF TEARS

Have you ever had a good cry? Maybe it is rare for you, or maybe it happens at the drop of a hat.

Have you ever wondered about the biology of tears?

Have you ever noticed the physical aspects of your emotional tears? Quivering abs? The prick of tears in your eyes? Chest tightening? Throat hurting? Nostrils flaring? Mouth crumpling?

Have you ever been scolded or criticized for crying?

Would it intrigue you to know that there are significant similarities between emotional tears and orgasms?

Join me to delve into this most baffling of human behaviors: the shedding of emotional tears or, as we know it in the vernacular, a "good cry."

Jayne Wesler has played many roles in her life. From the newsroom to the intense hush of psychotherapy sessions in various venues, including a locked psychiatric unit, to trying cases in courtrooms in Newark, Trenton, and Atlantic City, New Jersey, Ms. Wesler has been both witness to, and actor in, the most intense of human dramas. Trained by experts at GCU and NYU to use her emotions as a tool, Ms. Wesler taps into human experience to help educate and heal others. In this riveting exposé, Ms. Wesler illuminates the parallels between orgasm and emotional tears, thereby demonstrating a biological legitimacy to the need for a good cry. Just as sex is the all-time, one-and-only treatment for epididymal hypertension (commonly known as "blue balls"), a good cry is the only remedy for a frustrated and achy soul—a blue heart.

HURTS SO GOOD: AN ORGASM OF TEARS WORKBOOK

Learn how to deepen your most important relationships with exercises for emotional intimacy. You'll be surprised how much your trust and your love for yourself and your partner will deepen when you utilize the activities and exercises in this extraordinary book.

My tears are my gift to you.

They mean I trust you; I am making myself vulnerable to you; I am opening myself up to you; I am taking the risk of being hurt to deepen my bonds with you. Maybe even I love you.

For my mom, the incomparable Betty Theime:

How do you say "thank you" to someone for loving you unconditionally all your life, no matter what you do?

How do you say "thank you" to someone for giving you everything?

How do you say "thank you" to someone for always believing in you, no matter what?

How do you thank someone for the million acts of selfless kindness she has done for you? For the restraint she has exercised when you've done something wrong, broken the rules, acted thoughtlessly?

How can you possibly?

The answer is, really, you cannot.

But then you don't have to. Because mothers just love you anyway.

But that is precisely why you should tell her how deeply you love her. That there is no one else in the world like her, anywhere. That no one could ever take her place.

Thank you, Mom. I love you maybe more than words can convey. But words can try. And words should try. I love who you are. I love your gentle, steadfast strength. I love your courage and your indomitable spirit. I love that you spread goodness and kindness wherever you go. I love that when people find out I am your daughter they say, “Oh, I love Betty!” Everyone says that. Everyone. That’s because you are good to everyone, no matter who they are or what they’ve done. It’s just your way, letting God shine through you and touch other people’s lives. I know I am very lucky, very blessed, very fortunate, to have you for a mom. And you should know that.

You are my heart, my springboard, my bow. I am your arrow. I will strive to carry the right things into the future, to carry on the legacy of strength, kindness, and courage.

I will be honored.

With All My Love,

Your daughter,

Jayne

Table of Contents

Chapter: One

"Come back here, ya little bastard!" yelled TJ.

The butcher's knife glinted in his hand as TJ chased his seven-year-old son, Bill, and Bill's friend Julien through the backyard.

Horrified, six-year-old Beth watched from the boughs of an apple tree in the backyard. Her father was drunk—wasn't he always?

It was the rare occasion when TJ—Dr. Terence James Miller—was stone-cold sober, but he was a smart, funny guy when he was. He worked hard at his chiropractic practice, but it was slow going. Dr. Miller had established his office in Jackson, a city in southern Michigan. Home was a house he'd rented on a small farm, which included an orchard, on the outskirts of town.

Chiropractors were a virtually unknown species in 1937 Michigan. The locals were of two opinions: he was either a quack or a magician. Dr. Miller also ran the local newspaper in the evenings and on the weekend to make ends meet. He was a great healer in the office and a great storyteller in the newsroom. But when he was drunk—that was a different story.

Most of the time, Dr. Miller took his violent temper out on his wife, Ada. He was a big man—six-foot two and husky. His sandy-brown hair made him look boyish. Until he drank too much. At those times, which were all too frequent, Beth, Bill, and 10-year-old Carolyn were well-acquainted with the sound of Dr. Miller's fists landing somewhere on Ada's body and with her cries for help. But if Ada wasn't available to be Dr. Miller's punching bag, anyone within arm's length would do.

Today was no exception. Luckily, the boys ran faster than Dr. Miller's drunken legs could carry him. They escaped through the back orchard, where Beth remained sheltered in the gnarly branches, while Dr. Miller tripped over a root and lay where he'd fallen. The orchard was silent except for the bees buzzing around the ripe apples as Beth climbed down to see whether he'd fallen on his knife, or it was simply his drunkenness keeping him grounded. Mean and violent though he was, Beth loved him. Maybe if she could be a good little girl, as he said, he wouldn't get drunk and hurt them.

But Dr. Miller had not impaled himself on the butcher's knife. He lay sprawled in the grass, still clad in his suit pants and a white shirt. He would live to bring the family more heartache—but only some. Beth's mother was no picnic either. Small, dark, and shapely, with a quick but hard laugh, Ada Miller waitressed for a living. She could've been a homemaker if TJ hadn't pissed away everything he'd earned. But Ada as a homemaker probably would have been a disaster as was everything else in their lives. Ada was no homebody. When not working or being beaten by her husband, she'd go out drinking, smoking, and playing cards with her friends. She rarely bothered to cook dinner, which meant the Miller kitchen was often cold, dark, and unwelcoming. Not that there was much to cook during the years of the Great Depression. The family often subsisted on ears of corn served steaming on a large platter. Money and food were scarce.

The plight of Ada's children didn't seem enough to motivate her to mend her ways although Beth was only 6. In Ada's mind, Carolyn was old enough to watch her brother and sister and keep house when Ada wasn't there.

Carolyn was well-suited to that task though she didn't relish it. Tall and sturdy, Carolyn had leadership qualities. In other words, she was bossy and frequently gave orders to her younger siblings. Bill, stocky and tall for his age, was the only boy, so he escaped housework. Barely old enough to attend school, Beth was a pretty child with brunette hair, clear skin, and intelligent eyes. Although she rarely had a reason to display it, she had a beautiful smile. Unfortunately, these qualities did nothing to endear her to her drunken father or absent mother. In short, 6-year-old Beth was nobody's darling.

Chapter: Two

BANG! The front door swung violently open and bounced off the living room wall, the doorknob deepening a hole in the sheetrock.

"Ada!" roared Dr. Miller. "Where's my dinner?"

Beth leaped up from the bed, where she was playing with her doll, and crouched, ready to run. Bill was seated at the desk, jammed against the wall, and Carolyn was sitting on the bed. Both had been doing their homework. The three children were in the small back bedroom, where they all slept in one double bed. Now they exchanged uneasy looks. They'd been down this road before.

There *was* no dinner. There *was* no Ada. She was out and about; the children had no idea where. Even though they hadn't done anything wrong, they knew they might pay a price.

Dr. Miller made his way into the kitchen, his tan, pin-striped suit jacket hanging open. He slammed open the cabinets and muttered to himself. Beth heard the *thunk*! of a plate and the chink of utensils hitting the table. Next came the *whoomph*! of suction—he'd pulled open the refrigerator door.

At least there's food in there tonight, Beth thought. Cold meatloaf and baked potatoes would help appease the monster in the kitchen.

Beth and her siblings remained silent. Anything they said or did would certainly be used against them, but it wouldn't be in a court of law. It would be right here at the hands of the only rule that prevailed in their home: their father's. He often meted out his brand of justice, and that was usually with a jaundiced eye. It's hard to judge things clearly when you're soused to the gills on whiskey.

On one rare occasion, the kids found Ada at home after they had trekked the long miles from the schoolhouse. There were no school buses in rural Michigan in 1937. The three of them clunked in through the doorway, dusty and tired. Seeing their mother sitting at the kitchen table with a strange woman, they stopped so abruptly that they bumped into each other.

"Ah, the kids are home! Edie, these are my children."

Shocked to see their mother home and in the kitchen, the three children remained motionless and staring. Beth wondered why her mother was putting a fake smile on her face and a cheerful note in her voice. This only added to the surreal nature of the moment.

Ada waved her arm at the kids in a come-here gesture, a lit cigarette wedged between two fingers trailing smoke. "Beth, come over here."

Beth walked cautiously to the table. Beth never knew when Mom would smack her face and she'd end up on the floor with a bloody lip. Beth was obedient but her antennae were up.

Looking at Edie, a wiry woman in a red-checked gingham dress with a white belt, Ada exclaimed, "Edie, would you look at those feet? Have you ever seen such big feet on a girl?"

The women looked at each other and laughed. They either didn't notice or didn't care about the hot flush that ran up Beth's neck, chest, and face. Her stomach knotted and her gaze fell to the floor. She stood there, ashamed, until her mother carelessly waved her away.

Chapter: Three

Bong! Bong! Ding dong, ding ding dong!

The bells of St. Mary Star of the Sea rang out from their tower. Sonorous and commanding, with a dash of mystery, they announced the Sunday-morning Mass in Latin. Located three blocks from the north branch of the Grand River in Jackson, Michigan, St. Mary's Byzantine towers faced west from their perch on the corner of Wesley and Mechanic streets.

Carolyn, Bill, and Beth, dressed in their best, walked to the church together. For some inexplicable reason, Ada insisted the children attend mass every Sunday morning, while she stayed home with her coffee and cigarettes.

Beth didn't mind. The Mass was an oasis in her dodgy young life, where unexpected troubles often sprang out to frighten her—or worse. Sunday morning was a joy and a celebration even though most of the service was over her head. On Saturday night, Beth was permitted a bath, which left her feeling soft and clean. Happiness welled up in her heart, and she was grateful for the warm water and cake of soap even though she was the last child to use the same bathwater. To top off this soaring sensation, Beth was allowed to wear her best dress, shoes, and bonnet (all hand-me-downs from Carolyn). Best of all was the time away from her tumultuous home life and the prize of calm, peace, and structure bestowed on her by the Catholic Mass.

The church's interior was beautiful. The stained-glass windows told stories: Mary holding the baby Jesus. Jesus as a young adult tipping over the tables of the moneychangers in the temple. Jesus on his knees, praying in the garden of Gethsemane. Christ hanging on the cross, wearing nothing but a cloth draped over his loins. The gilt-edged paintings on the soaring ceiling struck awe into Beth's heart. And then there was the statue of the Blessed Virgin, whose face looked so peaceful it gave Beth hope that her own mother might someday love her and be kind to her.

Beth slipped into the wooden pew next to Carolyn, and Bill pushed in after her. After the first hymn was sung, people murmured around her. As soon as the processional began, however, a reverent hush fell over the congregation.

Beth loved the pageantry of the processional. It was like a parade but more beautiful and more mysterious. More powerful somehow. Beth could *feel* it. First came Mr. Gallant, the director of St. Joseph's bank, carrying the gold processional cross—eight feet tall if it was an inch—with a figure of Christ nailed onto it. It made Beth's heart pound for reasons she didn't understand.

Next came a man carrying the Book of the Gospels, a large scarlet tome bound in gold leaf. Beth's eyes grew even rounder as she took it all in. Last came Father Flynn, resplendent in his purple-and-gold chasuble. Beth thought it was the most marvelous costume ever—better even than what the nuns got to wear although Beth adored the nuns and loved to see them smiling at her.

Father Flynn delivered the gospel reading for the day from the Book of John. Tall and authoritative, Father Flynn's sonorous voice boomed into the sanctuary: "This is My commandment, that you love one another as I have loved you. Greater love hath no man than this, that a man lay down his life for his friends."

Beth was confused. *What about his children?* she thought. *Shouldn't a man love his children more than his friends?* But she didn't want to make God angry by questioning His word. She knew what happened when you made Father angry. Maybe if she prayed hard enough, was good and obedient enough, her parents would call her their darling girl and cook her dinner and stay home at night and stop fighting.

Soon the movement and flow of the mass restored Beth's peace. When Father Flynn got to the sermon, young Beth found herself riveted. He talked about overcoming something called *adversity*.

"Today we need words of encouragement," his voice rang out from the pulpit. "When you are faced with adversity, don't turn away. Accept it. Find gratitude in your heart and learn to embrace it."

Beth didn't know what *adversity* was, but she studied the faces of the adults around her. They were paying attention. Maybe because Father Flynn didn't often speak this way.

"Let us lean on God and on one another to overcome the insufficiencies of our families of origin, and to leap the hurdles and dodge the bullets life throws at us."

Even though Beth didn't know what *insufficiencies* were, she had a feeling her family had plenty of them. She did know what hurdles and bullets were, though, and she could picture what he was saying. She felt a stirring in her heart and an unfamiliar sense of hope.

"Grasp the planets and turn around, not just your own life's trajectory," intoned Father Flynn, "but your children's and grandchildren's as well."

Beth's eyes opened wide. Was this really possible? How did you grasp the planets? How did you turn around your *trajectory*, whatever that was? Beth's brows furrowed. She had questions in her mind and hope in her heart.

During the offering and response, everyone spoke in harmony, the priest beseeching and the people eager to respond.

"Have mercy on us, O Lord," called Father Flynn.

The congregants responded as one, "For we have sinned against you."

"Show us, O Lord, Your mercy," implored Father Flynn.

In one voice, the people chanted, "And grant us your salvation."

Beth didn't understand everything, but she felt it. Surely this calm, good place, and all of these people—the priest, the nuns, the congregation's families—knew something she didn't know. Here she felt safe. Here, no one would humiliate her or hurt her.

After singing "Holy, Holy, Holy" and the final prayer, Father Flynn brought the rite to a close: "The Mass has ended. You may now go in peace."

Beth stepped outside the church's tall, wooden doors into the March wind, which was sharp and tore at her clothing. Her coat had no buttons, so she pulled it close around her to stave off the chill.

Chapter: Four

Beth's sunny hope was soon blocked out by the storms that raged inside her home. Dr. Miller's drunken rages continued until Ada fled with the children to Benton Harbor, Michigan. Beth was frightened by all the changes. She felt lost and unsettled but believed her mother when Ada promised things would get better.

At least there were no drunken beatings. But other than a new school, there wasn't much else. No friends and a cold, empty apartment. Ada worked even more hours than she had when the family lived together in Jackson. That left Carolyn, Bob, and Beth home alone most of the time.

When Beth started third grade in Benton Harbor, the court granted Ada a divorce. Word got out and rumors spread. The community turned a cold shoulder to Ada, treating her like a loose woman. Divorce was rare in 1939. People didn't talk openly about domestic violence or alcoholism. You kept those things to yourself.

Ada's life was a slog. She worked back-to-back shifts at the local diner. The breakfast shift started at six and ended at 10. She returned to serve the lunch crowd from noon until 2 p.m., took a one-hour meal break, during which she read the paper, drank coffee, and smoked cigarettes. She was back on duty from 3 p.m. to 7 p.m. six days a week. On Sundays, Ada slept in. One of the kids would fetch her the Sunday paper and a pack of cigarettes. She'd shoo them off to Mass and tell herself that this made her a good mother. She was rewarded with peace and quiet.

Ada's schedule made it difficult to make new friends. The other waitresses were not welcoming. They were all single and talked about Ada behind her back. She'd occasionally hear part of a whispered conversation as she passed their hard eyes. Worse, they openly competed for the regular customers.

After a while, the hostile atmosphere, Ada's loneliness and fatigue and the way the community snubbed her made Ada rethink her position. The distance from Dr. Miller made her heart grow fonder and her memories of domestic violence fade. After a year of misery, Ada called TJ and the pair rekindled their romance. A brief telephone courtship ended in 1941, when they remarried. Ada and the children moved back to Jackson, and the union produced two more children: Priscilla Jean in January 1942 and Luke Thomas in May 1943.

Old patterns soon returned, however. After Ada suffered yet another horrifying beating—this one with a blackjack, which Beth and her siblings witnessed from the second-story landing—she'd had enough. The parents separated for good.

When Beth was in seventh grade, she, Ada, and her four siblings moved back to Benton Harbor, taking an apartment in a three-story house that belonged to a complex called Butler's Addition. Despite Ada's poor experience in that community, it felt familiar and safe. But their apartment was cramped, and although they had heat and electricity, they had no telephone.

Ada often left Priscilla, a toddler, and Luke, an infant, alone in a playpen when she went out. Luke would cry and cry, and Prissy would try to comfort him. The woman upstairs was supposed to watch them, but that never happened, and Ada never checked on it. When she came home from school, Beth would find Prissy and Luke home alone. Luke's diaper would be wet and cold. His bottom would be covered in a red rash, and snot would be running from his little nose. Both he and Prissy were wretched and inconsolable.

By this time, Beth was a leggy 12-year-old. She was strong and unconsciously graceful, yet she still felt like the little girl with big feet who could never make her parents happy. She saw herself as the big sister to Prissy and Luke, and so felt responsible for them, but she was unable to find a solution to their predicament. Luke's fear and longing, Prissy's terror, and her own helplessness took hold in Beth's psyche, and the cry of a baby forever afterward disturbed her.

Later that school year, Dr. Miller used his authority to take the children. He'd married again—a pitiless, pinch-faced woman named Edith. They lived on a farm in Jackson, Michigan, and grew vegetables, grapes, gooseberries, and fruit trees. They also raised chickens. Beth learned to pay close attention to the moods of her father and stepmother, particularly after one instance when Beth didn't respond immediately to Edith's call, and Edith had beaten her with a razor strap.

While this was traumatic, Beth realized that Edith was just as mean to her own daughter, Mavis, on whom she also whaled with the same strap. Beth took a small measure of consolation from knowing that Edith didn't hate her; she hated everyone. Her hatred marred them and left bruises all over their bodies. When they wore their bathing suits at the beach and people looked askance at them, Beth felt ashamed. She came to see her stepmother's hatred as stemming from her own shortcomings, and she sought to do better to make up for it.

During her time on the Jackson farm, Beth walked many miles to school, carrying her lunch pail. *Will we ever get there?* she wondered as she shifted the heavy metal lunchbox from one hand to another. It banged against her little legs until they were bruised and sore.

For her midday meal, she'd have two hunks of home-baked bread spread with a measly amount of peanut butter. No jelly to make it go down easier, and nothing to drink to wash it down. As dry as dust, like her loveless and comfortless life.

At the end of that school year, Beth's seventh-grade year, Ada showed up at school and said she was taking the kids to a fair. Instead, she kidnapped them, packing them off once again to the Benton Harbor apartment.

One night during that summer of 1944, Ada woke her 12-year-old daughter in the darkest hours of the morning and told her to get to a payphone and call the doctor. Ada then went back to bed, where she lay bleeding.

Beth was terrified. *I can't go down the path alone!* It was dark out, strange and menacing. Not like in the daytime. Even in the daytime, bullies sometimes hid on that sheltered path and picked on younger children. But in the dead of the night, it was a far different world.

And yet she didn't see how she could get out of it. She slipped out the front door and stood for a moment in the dark. The night silence bore down heavily. Beth walked a long, long way down the dark, empty street, cringing every time she heard a noise. She'd whip a glance over her shoulder, but nothing was ever there. Nothing visible, at least. Creepy vagabonds and evil men loomed large in her imagination, and she shivered.

Down the street, over the viaduct, and through the woods, but there was no kindly grandmother nearby to hold her hand, offer advice, smooth her dark hair from her worried brow, or come when she was needed. How had this become Beth's responsibility, to walk miles in the dead of night? But she had to go. Her mother had bidden her. Her mother was ill, and she needed the doctor. She needed Beth to get to a public telephone and summon him. Right away! Before … before what? Before she died? Beth's thoughts swirled around in a panic.

The dark secret buried in this event didn't emerge until years later: Ada had crossed state lines to have a back-alley abortion. It was a desperate thing to do, but everything was desperate then.

Despite the clandestine abortion, Ada soon recovered and began looking for a better job in a better town. She and the children moved again, renting an apartment in a house on Pine Street in St. Joseph. A quaint town along Lake Michigan with brick streets and sidewalks, "St. Joe" was a step up for the Millers. Ada landed a better-paying job in a Victorian lakeside resort.

Despite the different locales and the "fresh starts," life for Beth remained the same. Absent father, absent mother, cold hearth, and a deep sense of loneliness. Of being nobody's darling.

Chapter: Five

Flames roared, snapped, and spit as the fire spread, burning through the timber and walls of the three-story house. Smoke seeped through every crack in the walls and ceiling. Beth woke with a start, heart pounding. She ran to her mother, who was still sound asleep.

"Wake up! Wake up!" she yelled as she shook Ada awake. "The house is on fire!"

Beth expected her mother to leap from the bed and usher all the children outside. But Ada was groggy and unresponsive.

Is she drunk again?

"Wake up! The house is on fire! We have to get out!"

Ada blinked several times, looking at Beth as if she were trying to focus. Finally, she sat up slowly, until her back was against the battered, upholstered headboard. Her unresponsiveness made Beth even more frantic.

"C'mon! C'mon!" she shrieked, jumping up and down on her bare feet.

Ada jerked upright and seemed to connect with reality. The heat of the flames swelled, and the air was thick with smoke.

Ada jumped from the bed, grabbing Beth's hand.

"Bill! Carolyn!" Ada cried as she scooped little Luke from his bed.

The older kids came running as Beth grabbed Priscilla Jean's hand. In the hallway outside the door of their apartment, the smoke was so thick they could hardly see. Coughing uncontrollably, Beth lifted Prissy into her arms, her eyes burning. She staggered under her sister's weight. A rafter crashed into the hallway behind them. Panic gripped her throat as she thought, *We're gonna die here!*

Strong hands seized her from behind. *Bill!*

Bill grabbed Priscilla Jean and pushed Beth forward. "Run!"

Out on the street, the family clung together. The fire reared up before them, three stories in the air, moaning and roaring like a red-and-orange monster, angrily tearing through their home, seeking retribution for past injustices, taking no prisoners, and inflicting a searing punishment on anyone who got in the way. The neighbors and residents of the upstairs and downstairs apartments watched in horror as the fire ate their Pine Street home alive.

Fire trucks roared to the scene, sirens wailing and bells clanging. Firemen dashed to attach hoses to the pump truck as two men apiece handled the powerful pipes. The gushing trails of water fountained up and over the three-story roof. But it was all for naught. The firemen had barely begun the fight when the whole structure collapsed in a dramatic pile, sending sparks and flames into the night sky.

After the fire, Ada and the children stayed with friends, Ben and Mary Stephens and Mary's son, Eugene, who lived in St. Joseph. This was Mary's second marriage. Her first marriage had been to a man who owned a line of grocery stores. The divorce settlement had left her and Eugene with a large home and a bottomless checkbook. Mary took great delight in sharing her ex-husband's wealth with friends old and new.

The fire had left Ada and the children with just the clothing on their backs. Mary's and Ben's offer to live in their grand five-bedroom lakefront home was a godsend. Ada had her own room; Bill and Luke shared another; and Carolyn, Beth, and Priscilla a third.

After the fire, Beth, who'd just turned 14, had started ninth grade in St. Joseph's High, a Roman Catholic school, where a particular nun inspired and motivated her.

Sister Marie Martha was young, happy, and fun-loving. With her blue eyes and strawberry-blond hair—detectable only when stray locks escaped from her wimple—Sister Marie was a natural beauty. She projected warmth and love, and Beth felt drawn to her. She was so kind. Just looking at Sister Marie, Beth felt a deep ache in her heart, a terrible longing for someone to love her just as she was: a lonely child who'd felt unwanted and unseen, now a young woman who craved a pure love. At times like that, Beth was overcome with a deep desire for Sister Marie to hold her while she let go of all the pain and fear in a great weeping catharsis. She longed for such a release even though she didn't understand it. What she wanted more than anything was to be loved. For a parent to love her enough to take the time to talk with her, to cook her a hot meal, to be gentle and kind.

Sister Marie was unique, but all the sisters at St. Joseph's made the students feel special and capable. They had a positive outlook on things, a natural curiosity and grasp of their subject matter. They passed this on to their students, and Beth thrived under their tutelage, like a young plant in the warm spring sunshine.

All the nuns at the school were positive and sunny. This was an outlook to which Beth had yet to be exposed. Day by day, Beth found her heart and mind growing by leaps and bounds.

Friendship found Beth, too. On her first day at St. Joe's, Beth had known no one and at lunchtime had taken a seat in the cafeteria by herself. She pulled her peanut-butter sandwich out of its wrapper and took a bite. Feeling self-conscious, she kept her head down while she ate.

A whirlwind of fragrant energy plopped down on the bench next to her.

"Hi, there! You're new, aren't you?"

Beth looked up to see a cheerful, smiling girl with pin-straight, blond hair and freckles.

"I'm Barbara. I wish I had curly hair like yours."

The girls chattered like magpies and became fast friends. Barbara was a popular student, and she introduced Beth to her circle of friends. Pretty soon, Beth felt as if she'd always been part of their group. She felt more grounded and confident.

Beth blossomed so much at St. Joe's that she even won a spot on the cheerleading squad. Her deep-blue cheer sweater with its gold lettering showed off her tiny waist and dark hair, and her short, pleated, blue skirt revealed her graceful legs. She'd never had a cute outfit like this before. Now that she lived with the Stephenses, she saw a father who went out to work every morning and returned in the evening, sober. Beth felt happier and more settled than ever before. Making friends with the other cheerleaders was icing on the cake. Who would've thought that losing your home and all your belongings could make you happier?

Standing on the sidelines of the football field, Beth's pulse raced as she cheered for the football team. Her heart swelled with pride as she and the other girls called out in the crisp afternoon air every Saturday.

Chick a lacka chick a lacka boom boom boom!

Chick a lacka chick a lacka boom boom boom!

Beth, Barbara, and the others grinned at each other as they executed their movements, accentuated with blue and yellow pompons. The crowd's roar as the team ran onto the field was so loud it reverberated in Beth's chest.

One day toward the end of Beth's freshman year, Ben and Mary announced their decision to move to New Jersey.

"New Jersey has great schools." Mary nodded at them over dinner. "You're welcome to come with us and stay with us there."

Mary saw herself as the patron saint of all her friends. Her philanthropy was amply funded by her ex-husband, the grocery king. The other side of that coin was, by spending the money, Mary was really sticking it to her ex. Mary's new husband, Ben, was easy-going and sociable, and he slavishly adored Mary, so he went along with all of her decisions.

The thought of losing all she had gained was painful and left Beth feeling empty and helpless. Where she had once been resigned to a life that didn't offer her much, the days at St. Joe's with Barbara and their friends had lit something fresh inside of her. The thought of being torn away from the first good thing she ever had—her school, Barbara, the other girls, cheerleading, and Sister Marie—left her with a hollow feeling in the pit of her stomach.

Beth tried to come to terms with this new development. Now that things were on the upswing for her at St. Joe's, she felt energized to go to school in the morning, to study, and to socialize. She didn't want to leave, but she liked living with the Stephenses.

The decision was soon made for her. Without consulting her children's feelings, Ada threw in her lot with Ben and Mary. Good riddance, Michigan!

One sunny Saturday in mid-June, they packed up the Stephenses' 1940 Buick Super Estate Wagon, and off they went. The day before they left, Beth had said a tearful good-bye to Barbara. They crossed their hearts and promised to write. It was a tight squeeze with Beth, her mother, and four siblings, Mary Stephens, her son, Eugene, and Ben at the wheel. Mary made all the kids sit in the back. That meant four teens on the bench seat with Luke on Beth's lap and Prissy on Carolyn's. Beth's legs were numb before they left Michigan. The hours on the road were endless. Everyone was stiff and staring.

The crew finally arrived at the home the Stephenses had rented on the corner of I Street and 18th Avenue in West Bank, New Jersey. The two-story home had dormers, a large porch, and a wide front yard. Though it had only four bedrooms, it accommodated everyone comfortably (Eugene bunked in the same room as Bill and Luke).

Beth transferred her new-found confidence along with her transcripts to her new school, Manasquan High, and kept the momentum she'd gained at St. Joe's going. As a sophomore, Beth was considered an upperclassman, which bestowed a certain amount of respect on her. In addition, her brilliant smile, svelte figure, and friendly nature made her popular. Not only did she make new friends and join the cheerleading squad, but she also got good marks across the board.

English and Science were her best subjects. So good, in fact, that her English teacher invited her to write for the school newspaper. Pretty soon, a local photographer was taking her picture in the library after the *Asbury Park Press* published an article she'd written. Lively and popular, Beth was delighted that her new friends gathered at her new home.

New Jersey's culture did carry some surprises for Beth. One Saturday a few of her girlfriends suggested they go to Vic's Italian Restaurant in Belmar.

"We'll order tomato pie. You'll love it." Dotty clapped excitedly.

That sounds disgusting, thought Beth, but she was too polite to say so.

Next thing she knew, Beth was delicately biting a steamy slice of pizza, fragrant with oregano and spicy tomato sauce. *I've never been so happy to be so wrong about something in my entire life,* she thought.

Life in New Jersey wasn't all fun and games, however. Ada hadn't been able to find a good job. She pined for the waitressing position—and the paycheck—she'd had at the upscale resort back in Jackson. Impatient and dreaming of the greener grass on the other side of the fence, Ada was soon making plans to return to Michigan with Beth's siblings—Beth didn't want to go back. She'd kept in touch with her first real friend, Barbara, from St. Joseph. They wrote to each other regularly and would remain pen pals for life. It was there on the page that Beth could pour out her heart. Despite this close relationship, which grounded Beth, she didn't want to pick up that life again. Even though Mary Stephens wasn't any better a housekeeper or cook than her own mother, Beth's life was still better in

New Jersey. At least there were no scenes filled with drunken screaming or violence.

Staying with Ben and Mary didn't solve all the problems, however. Mary Stephens wasn't much use in the kitchen. This drove Eugene to make stacks of ketchup sandwiches. Despite Mary's generosity in housing Beth and her family, her hospitality stopped there. Mary was particularly inattentive to mundane chores like grocery shopping and cleaning the house. After her mother left for Michigan, Beth had no money—Mary provided no allowance—and there was no food in the house.

Out of desperation and with virtually no parental oversight, 15-year-old Beth dropped out of school and got a job at Berman's 5 & 10 variety store. She gave the Stephenses $5 every week out of her $14 paycheck. For Beth, life was predictable and safe. And that was good.

Even though she'd dropped out of school, Beth's friends still hung around. The teens would often play games, talk, or smoke cigarettes in the front yard. A young man named Donald Hoffman began to stop by. Donald was 23 and had served three years in the United States army. Short, with curly, dark hair and a trim waist, Don displayed his biceps in tight T-shirts. He invited Beth out on a date, and soon they were driving around most nights in Donald's car, listening to country music.

Chapter: Six

In September 1947, Donald bought Beth a beautiful locket for Beth's 16th birthday—a symbol of the deepening of their relationship. One night after riding around, they parked by the river and fell asleep. Unfortunately, it was a deep sleep. When Donald brought Beth home in the wee hours, the couple found that the Stephens had already called the police.

An uproar ensued, but instead of defending Beth, Donald went home, leaving her to deal with the fallout by herself. The Stephenses insisted the police take Beth to a doctor to be examined. Neither the Stephenses nor the police believed Beth, and they all intended to force her to undergo a vaginal exam to ensure she hadn't been "tampered with."

Two uniformed officers drove Beth to Dr. McGreevy's office, which was attached to his home, in the middle of the night. The doctor was none too happy at being roused from his bed for such a task. The officers remained in the waiting room while Dr. McGreevy brusquely ushered Beth into his examination room. It was very cold.

"Take off your clothing," he ordered.

Beth had never been naked in front of a man, yet here she was alone, innocent, and being treated like something less than human. Shaking, Beth unbuttoned her dress and pulled it off while he watched. She held the dress against her body, giving her thin protection from Dr. McGreevy's penetrating stare.

He yanked the dress from her grasp and threw it onto a chair. "Take off your slip and your underpants."

Beth stared at him, frozen in place.

"C'mon, hurry up, I don't have all night," he barked.

Mortified, Beth managed to fumble through the motions.

"Now lie down." He pointed to the exam table.

What happened next was unexpected and horrifying. Dr. McGreevy bent Beth's legs and placed them in the metal stirrups alongside the table. As he pushed a finger into her vagina, she bit back a cry and squeezed her eyes shut, trying to escape from this waking nightmare.

Dr. McGreevey withdrew and washed his hands at the sink. Beth lay, shaking, on the table. When he turned around and saw her, he said, "Well, what're you waiting for? Get up and get dressed." And he walked out.

Beth clambered off the table, drew her clothing back on, and joined the police in the waiting room. Her head hung low as Dr. McGreevey pronounced her a virgin, reassuring the police that she hadn't been tampered with.

He turned to Beth. "From now on, young lady," he said, putting a hand on her shoulder, "stay home at night. And don't go dating men who are older than you. Otherwise, you'll find yourself in real trouble."

With a nod, Dr. McGreevey showed them to the door.

As Beth got into the back of the police cruiser, she felt numb. She hadn't been raped, nor had she had sexual intercourse. She was intact. She had told the truth. She was pure as driven snow. Or had been, till they had soiled her in a way that she would never forget no matter how hard she tried.

News of Beth's virginity had no effect on Ben and Mary. They were angry with Beth for staying out all night with Donald. They found her behavior unacceptable, and they were concerned there'd be "talk" in the community. They thought Ada might blame them if Beth got "into trouble," so they were ready to send Beth back to Michigan.

But Beth didn't want to go. What would she have gone back to Michigan for? Ada was seeing a new boyfriend. For all Beth knew, they were living together. After what Beth had been through with the police and Dr. McGreevey, she didn't want to live in some transient lodging with an unknown man. She'd found the most stability with Mary and Ben Stephens. There was nothing and nowhere to go "home" to. Beth was contributing money to the household, and she continued to give the Stephenses money each week. Their angry recriminations soon died down.

That was the only thing that went back to normal in Beth's life. For her, the doubting of her integrity by the Stephenses and the police and the cold, rough, impersonal treatment at the hands of the doctor all reinforced the deepest belief that Beth harbored in her heart: She was nobody's darling. She felt worthless. She became apathetic and no longer cared about anyone or anything, especially not herself.

More and more, Beth withdrew from her friends. She got up, went to work, and that was it. She was in a downward spiral, mentally, physically, and emotionally. Lonely and neglected, she was vulnerable. When Donald pressured her to sleep with him, she gave in. What did it matter anymore? She'd already been violated by the very people who should have been her protectors. At least Donald held her, called her his sweetheart, and told her that he loved her.

In March 1948, Beth missed her period. When

Beth's pregnancy was confirmed in mid-April, Donald drove them to Elkton, Maryland, where they were married by a justice of the peace. Donald had yet to inform his own parents of this news, and the couple needed a place to stay.

When they returned from Maryland, Beth and Donald broke the news to Ben and Mary. Although angry, Ben kept his cool, but Mary ranted and raved.

"How could you do this to us?" Mary asked as she paced the living room, gesturing with her hands. She turned to look at Beth. "What will your mother think?" She spoke to Donald. "And you! You're an adult. We could file charges against you." Mary was working herself into a lather.

Ben spoke up. "Now, now, Mary. They're married now." He glanced at Donald. "I'm sure Don's gonna do right by her. Isn't that right, Don?"

In the end, the Stephenses allowed the couple to stay with them for the time being as long as they paid their rent and followed the house rules. Don didn't like it. He thought they were being treated like children, and things between the couples remained tense.

In May, when she was two months pregnant, Beth decided to go out to Michigan to inform her mother of her marriage and pregnancy face to face. Once again, Donald left Beth, 16 years old and pregnant, to deal with a difficult situation by herself. The journey by train was long and Beth had morning sickness. Still, she marveled at the different views she had from the train window.

When Beth arrived at the house where Ada was staying, her mother was in the middle of making apple butter. The whole kitchen was suffused with the smell of cinnamon and apples. Mason jars covered the table and the countertops, their glass surfaces winking and reflecting rainbows of light. Beth was momentarily overcome by this new homey side to Mother.

Unfortunately, the smell of apple butter and the lovely glow of the jars were the only inviting aspects of this home. Ada, Priscilla Jean, and Luke were living with more "friends." Ada and the wife had worked together at the lakeside resort, and Ada had run into her when she returned. Carolyn had enrolled in a business school and was living in a dorm, while Bill had joined the military.

Unfortunately, these "friends" lived in a dirty, cockroach-infested house on the wrong side of town. The husband patronized the neighborhood bars and regularly brought home his friends for a drink. Beth was worried about her younger brother and sister. She was especially worried about Prissy, a bright, blond, budding 11-year-old. Beth saw the way the men's eyes followed the cute, leggy little girl as she walked around the house.

As distressing as this was, Ada's insistence that Beth have an abortion was far worse.

"Mom, how could you even think that?"

"Easy. You're young and it's the only way out. Down the road, you'll thank me."

Beth was revolted. *This is my baby we're talking about.* "But I *want* this baby. I *love* this baby."

"Pssh." Ada flicked cigarette ashes into the ashtray. "Love. Where does that get you? You better do as I say, or you'll be sorry."

But Beth was adamant. This was her baby. Her child. She would care for her child and love her child. She would give her child the life and love she never had. Suddenly, Father Flynn's words from years ago came back to her: "Grasp the planets and turn around, not just your own life's trajectory, but your children's and grandchildren's as well."

She recalled the scripture verse that Father Flynn had read out that day: "This is My commandment, that you love one another as I have loved you. Greater love hath no man than this, that a man lay down his life for his friends." And she remembered thinking, *What about his children? Shouldn't a man love his children more than his friends?*

Beth would do that, she decided. She would find the strength, and she would lay down her life for her child.

Chapter: Seven

Donald, on the other hand, had no such lofty aspirations. He had not yet completely faced his impending fatherhood. Not only did he not tell his parents that Beth was pregnant, he didn't even inform them that he'd married her. Instead, he followed her to Michigan, where Ada had put her up. He got a job as a mechanic right away and quickly established a pattern of not coming home after work. Instead, he'd go out to have a beer with "the guys." He may have even been finding female company.

Donald was fit and attractive. He was also brooding and moody, the kind of man women often found themselves attracted to. He might have been fun to date, in a dangerous sort of way, but he wasn't the marrying kind. He didn't come home at the end of the day, help with the laundry, the cooking, the cleaning, or the diaper-changing. He put himself first and saw his masculine needs as superior to Beth's.

Donald had fallen in with his fellow mechanics. At the end of the day, Charlie, Harry, Jim, and Bill would punch the clock at the garage, pick up their lunch pails, and one of them would call out, "Hey, Donnie! Got time to grab a beer?"

Pretty soon, the five of them were sitting around a scarred table in Mahoney's, downing a few cold ones to smooth out the stress and irritation of the day. Donald was the new guy in the group, so he often got roasted. It was an initiation of sorts, a kind of a manly slap on the back. They also interrogated Donald about what had brought him from New Jersey out to Michigan. What could tear a person away from a town near the Atlantic Ocean? They'd heard about the beaches and the ocean's beauty and thought he was crazy for leaving. Charlie, Jim, Harry, and Bill were all in their late 20s and early 30s. They knew Donald was a baby, but when they found out his wife was 16, they laughed uproariously.

"Robbing the cradle, eh, Donnie?

"Looking for some young, fresh thing to keep you warm at night? Good one. Get 'er pregnant and she won't go nowhere."

When they found out Beth had traveled to Michigan alone on the train, ahead of Donald, they laughed even harder.

"Oooh, she's trying to get away from you, Donnie boy."

"Ha, she left you already!" Jim guffawed and lifted the amber liquid to his lips as suds ran down the side.

Beth was in the kitchen of the hovel, scrambling eggs in a frying pan. Her dark hair was pulled back and she wore an apron over her dress. Although it was late May and the days were getting longer, this late in the evening, the single bulb hanging over the two-burner stove offered only dim light. Maybe it was better that way: Beth couldn't see the cockroaches scuffling in the shadows. She had scrubbed and cleaned the kitchen and the bathroom, but the pests persisted.

She jumped when the screen door slammed behind her. A memory of her drunken father banging into the house had given her a momentary fright. She turned to find Donald scowling at her, eyes bloodshot from the alcohol.

"Where've you been?" Beth asked.

"Can't a man stop by for a cold one after a long, hot day at work?"

"It'd be nice to know when my husband was coming home from work."

Donald ignored her remark. "What's for dinner?'

"Egg sandwiches."

“Jesus Christ!” he roared. “What kind of dinner is that?”

“The kind you’re getting tonight. It’s all we have.”

Donald slammed back through the door, leaving Beth alone with the cockroaches and the scrambled eggs.

Chapter: Eight

Beth sat in a pool of lamplight.

Ada and Ada's friend Martha sat nearby, playing cards and drinking cocktails. Occasionally, Ada sucked on a Chesterfield, which she then returned to the ashtray at her elbow. "Where's Donnie tonight?"

"He went out." Beth didn't feel like talking about it.

"That's a man for you. Get you pregnant then take off." Ada sounded as if she were speaking from experience, but Dr. Miller never took off; he came home ugly, drunk, loud, and violent. If he had taken off, it might've been better, since he had come close to beating Ada into a coma on several occasions.

"He went out for a walk." Beth didn't know why she was defending Donald.

Martha and Ada exchanged a look.

Did he get *me pregnant? Wasn't* I *involved in that decision? On the other hand,* Beth thought, *I don't want a marriage like Mom and Dad's.* She glanced out the window into the darkness. *Mom wants me to stay here. Maybe I should stay. By myself.*

Beth leapt suddenly to her feet. "Why are you lumping my husband together with all other men?" Beth stood rigid in the middle of the room, hands curled into fists. "Do you think I had nothing to do with getting pregnant? Maybe I wouldn't have gotten pregnant if you and Dad had ever taken proper care of us."

With that, Beth whirled around, stalked into the adjoining bedroom, and slammed the door.

Ada raised her brows, tapped the excess ash off her cigarette, and dealt the next round.

Donald's nightly habit of having a beer on the way home continued. Soon it morphed into a second pattern of behavior: he'd come home late, eat, and go back out. Sometimes the excuse was, "I need cigarettes."

Four hours later she was still waiting. *That's some long trip to get cigarettes. I know the stores are on the other side of town, but you don't have to go to Indiana.* But no matter what she thought, she never said anything more.

In truth, she blamed herself for getting pregnant. That was the subtle message embedded in society in the 1940s: nice girls waited until they got married to sleep with someone. Or, if you did sleep with a man, you had the brains not to get pregnant.

She also had a deep-seated belief in her inability to be loved. *There must be something wrong with me*, she often thought but never said it out loud. After all, other people had normal families. Fathers and mothers lived together in harmony, with respect for one another without getting drunk and beating the living daylights out of each other. *It must be genetic,* she thought. But it was also unfair.

If she'd been a better wife—older, prettier, more interesting—would Donald come straight home from work? Would he stay home in the evenings? What was she doing wrong?

Donald was talking about heading back to New Jersey. He was tired of living in Michigan in a filthy hovel with Ada and her friends. He missed his brothers. He didn't want to find a place of their own and make the move permanent. He'd had a good job in New Jersey, and he wanted to go back to it. He grew increasingly irritable and impatient.

Beth wasn't too happy living in this hellhole, either. She cleaned the kitchen and the bathroom and did the laundry. No matter how often she scrubbed and tidied, though, the family's slovenly habits soon returned the place to its typical condition.

Beth had tried to find work as a store clerk or a waitress, but no one wanted to hire a pregnant 16-year-old. The house was depressing, and her mother's friends were creepy. Ada herself was hardly ever home. Why should she stay? What was there for her?

At other times, however, Beth thought she should stay. Since she was home most of the time, she could monitor Luke and Prissy. Beth was a buffer between them and the bad things that might happen to them, the things that had already happened to Beth.

During her stay with Ada and her buddies, Beth met her high school friend, Barbara, at a coffee shop. When she arrived and saw Barbara already seated, Beth felt her nervousness ease. She hadn't known she was so stressed. After a hug and some rapid-fire conversation to catch up with one another, they got down to business.

"So, are you back in Michigan for good?" Barbara asked. Then her gaze fell on Beth's wedding band. "Oh, my goodness!" she exclaimed. "You'd better tell me everything.

And Beth did. All about the pregnancy test, the whirlwind elopement to Maryland, her trip out to tell her mother. Then, with her gaze downcast, she admitted, "Don didn't come out with me. He had me tell my mother first, then he came out and got a job. The trouble is, he goes out to the bars after work, comes home to eat dinner, and goes back out again." Beth looked at Barbara. "I don't know what to do. If he really loved me, he'd want to spend more time with me." Her hand fell on her abdomen. "Especially now."

Barbara reached over and took Beth's hand. "That's a lot of changes for both of you," she said. "Give it some time. Things should straighten out. You'll adjust."

Looking back on that advice, Beth hoped that was true. *Greater love hath no man …* she would think. Should she lay down her life for her siblings and her child and stay in Michigan? Or was going back to New Jersey the right thing to do? Was that laying down her life for her child—returning to New Jersey with her husband and making a life there?

Beth paced the small bedroom. Her mother and siblings were sleeping in the twin beds. Beth's eyes fell on her mother's things on the small vanity table against the far wall. Light from a streetlamp fell on Ada's cosmetics. Beth jerked the cushioned chair back and propped herself on it, peering into the shadowy mirror.

Who was she, really? Was she pretty enough to hold Don's interest? Or any man's?

Grabbing a tube of red lipstick, Beth hurriedly traced the full outline of her lips and filled them in with abandon. A thin line of liquid black followed along her upper lash line. Beth paused, then flicked on a subtle wing at the end, mimicking a cat's eye. In a dramatic finish, she dabbed face powder all over with the soft pouf, then gazed deeply at herself in the mirror.

Suddenly, Beth struck out blindly, swiping the cosmetics to the floor, where they landed with a crash. Resting her head on her arm, she let the warm, salty tears roll down her face, smearing the makeup in black rivulets.

A little voice in the dark made her hold her breath.

"Mom?" Prissy whispered softly. "Is that you?"

"Oh, no, sweetheart." Beth rushed to quiet Priscilla before Luke woke up too. "No, it's just me, your silly big sister. C'mon, I'll lie down with you." She pulled Prissy into a spoon snuggle where the girl fell fast asleep.

Not knowing where else to turn for comfort, Beth closed her eyes and prayed, more fervently than ever, for direction.

Chapter: Nine

In early June, the sun rose over a balmy St. Joseph as Beth sat looking out the living room window. She'd been awake for hours; she hadn't slept much at all. Donald had gone out after dinner, which had been Beth's first attempt at meatloaf and mashed potatoes. Given his reaction, it appeared she hadn't done such a good job of it.

But how would I know if he liked it? She wondered. *He's always so moody, and he never talks anymore. Maybe once he could just smile at me and say, "Thank you."*

As the sky brightened, Beth felt a resolution forming in her heart. She was having a baby. *They* were having a baby. They had to do it *together*. If Donald would be happier in New Jersey, then that's where they would put down their roots, the roots of their new family.

Ada wasn't happy when Beth informed her of her decision, but neither did it bother her a great deal. She just shrugged with a *c'est la vie* attitude. "It's your life. You have to live it the way you want."

When Donald's car was packed with their few belongings, Beth hugged her brother and sister, told them to be good and study hard, and to write to her. On the doorstep, Ada took Beth's hands and pressed something into them. Looking down, Beth saw her mother's wooden rosary beads.

"Take these with you. You'll make better use of them than I ever did."

This kind of tender moment was so unusual it left Beth speechless. Suddenly, all Beth's doubts swirled to the surface, and she grabbed her mother in a tight, quick hug.

"Take care of yourself, Mother. I'll miss you." She turned to go without a backward glance, determined to leave like an adult. It was only when she was in the car that Beth let her tears flow. They rolled down her face in rivulets, dampening the collar of her jacket. Donald glanced over at her, then reached over and patted her knee. At this uncharacteristic kindness, her heart swelled with happiness, and she felt determined to make her marriage and motherhood a success. She looked ahead at the road unspooling in front of her and took in all the bright colors.

Chapter: Ten

Donald drove the last nail into the last shingle and straightened up. He surveyed the roof of the little, white stucco house he'd just completed and felt a mixture of relief and pride. His pregnant young wife had helped him put up the walls and haul concrete blocks, 2 x 4s, and plywood. Until she hurt herself, that is. Damn woman. Lucky for him his family had rallied around him—if not around his wife—and his brothers Ryan and George had come over every weekend and some evenings to help finish the job. Although Ryan and George knew the truth—Beth had been a guileless virgin when she met Don, and Don had participated fully and happily in getting her pregnant—Don's parents believed that Beth had trapped him into marriage.

Don had purchased a small lot about six miles from his parents' home and around the corner from his brother, Ryan, in Wall Township, New Jersey. Wall was a rural area about five miles from the town of Belmar, and ten miles from the closest city, Asbury Park. Don's brother George also lived in Wall, just a few miles away. Don was close to his brothers if not to his wife.

Don's lot sat on Belmar Boulevard, a country highway, in between a farm market and a hardware store. Belmar Boulevard divided two sprawling, blue-collar neighborhoods. The houses were small to mid-size, the yards neat and tidy. Big Daddy Rod's gas station sat on the corner a block away. Big Daddy was a character. Loquacious and outgoing, he dressed in oddball outfits with mismatched patterns. Polka dots with checks. Stripes with herringbone. No neutral colors either. Everything was loud. He was married to a respectable woman but had an eye for the ladies. Everyone thought he was all talk and no action. He gave the neighborhood its local color. Next to Big Daddy's gas station was the pharmacy and a local mom-and-pop shop.

Donald shook his head unconsciously. He still felt trapped by the turn his life had taken. He'd never gotten anyone pregnant before, and he'd gotten plenty of action in his late teens and early twenties. He'd done two years in the Army, from December 1944 to December 1946, during the Asiatic Pacific Campaign. He'd been honorably discharged at the rank of sergeant.

There'd been plenty of women in foreign and domestic ports. He'd never gotten anyone pregnant before. Why did it have to be this 17-year-old girl? She was beautiful and kind, he admitted to himself, but holy cow, a man had one life to live. He wanted to live it before he died. He'd already served during the war, or "conflict," as they called it. He didn't want to serve more time shackled to a woman and kids.

But here he was, building a house to shelter his family. Beth had given birth to baby Barbara two days ago.

Beth and their daughter were due to come home in a few days, so Don was here, making the best of it. He was taking on the responsibilities of a husband and a father, but he didn't have to like it. And he didn't have to be perfect. Maybe he could have his cake and eat it, too—make the best of it in other ways.

On that thought, Donald climbed down the ladder, showered, dressed, and dabbed on a little aftershave. He'd go down to the local watering hole and see what his prospects were.

Chapter: Eleven

The days after Beth came home from the hospital were among the hardest of her life—and that was saying something. In the beginning, Beth kept baby Barbara in a bassinet next to the bed. The baby was hungry every two hours. Beth was breastfeeding but very unsure of herself. Donald yelled if the baby woke him during the night. That only made her cry harder, made Donald angrier, and made Beth more nervous.

It was a vicious cycle. After a week, Beth moved Barbara into her own bedroom. Beth was a light sleeper and would wake at Barbara's slightest fussing, even from the next room. Problem solved. At least it solved Donald's interrupted sleep. Beth was sleeping on pins and needles, afraid she'd sleep through a feeding. She was more tired than she'd ever been in her life.

But she was happy, too. Beth had named the baby "Barbara" after her friend. Having a smart, kindhearted, and beautiful namesake gave her baby some connection in life, Beth thought. For Beth's part, having a baby in 1948 at the age of seventeen years and six weeks was daunting, especially since she had an indifferent mother and no visiting nurse to impart words of wisdom to her. It was trial and error. Her in-laws were of no help even though Donald was one of 10 children. Peter and Ethel Hoffman remained stern and uncommunicative. They seemed to blame Beth for Donald's failure to inform them that he'd gotten married or that his new wife was with child. They gave no support to the young wife and mother.

In addition to adjusting to motherhood, Beth had to clean the house, do the laundry, cook dinners that Donald liked, and sew all the clothing. Never had she felt so wholly unprepared for anything in her life.

After Beth was home for a couple of weeks, Mary Stephens came for a visit. She clucked over Barbara in her bassinet but didn't pick her up. Dressed in a fancy red dress and black pumps, her short hair styled, Mary looked as if she were going out on a date instead of visiting a newborn. She sat on the sofa in the living room as Beth made some coffee.

Mary took out a cigarette and lit it. Blowing smoke out the side of her mouth, she asked, "So, how are you doing? Is the baby sleeping at night?"

Beth's brows furrowed as she shook her head.

"No, not yet. I have to feed her every two hours. I'm nursing her."

"Nursing her! Good lord, Beth! Give that child some formula. It'll help her sleep through the night."

Beth thought little Barbara might be too young to sleep through the night, but she bit her tongue. The truth was, she was so happy to have some company, she didn't mind that Mary gave her unwanted advice. After all, Beth was only 17! Mary was older, and she'd been through this before. It was almost like having a mother.

The visit lasted a scant 30 minutes because Mary had to get to an appointment, she said. Beth didn't see her again for weeks.

A lesser person might have broken down, but Beth had made up her mind: She would lay her life down for this baby, for her family. She would grasp the planets and change the trajectory of her life, especially her child's life. She could do it. She had to. She did not want this beautiful baby to grow up feeling as unloved and as worthless as she had.

And this baby *was* beautiful. Her hair was golden; her skin was luminous porcelain; and her little rosebud mouth was a beautiful, deep pink. Beth never knew you could love anyone so much. The labor had been long and painful, and Beth had gone through it alone—

again. But everything had changed in the delivery room. She'd been pushing and pushing when the doctor called for her to stop.

"It's a girl!" he said.

Beth was delighted even though she knew Donald had wanted a son. A little girl. How exciting! She would hold her and rock her and love her and teach her everything. This little girl would never feel unloved, never feel as if she were nobody's darling.

She's my *darling,* Beth thought. It was a vow and a declaration of love.

When Barbara was six weeks old, Beth and Donald took her to St. Rose Roman Catholic Church in Belmar for her christening. Donald was grumpy but went along with it. No one from his family came. They claimed to be Methodists but never set foot in church. Ben and Mary came with Eugene and stood with Beth at the altar. Mary had given Beth a sweet baptismal gown with a cap and tiny, white leather shoes for Barbara to wear. Beth thought Barbara looked like a little doll in her new outfit.

The church was shadowy and cold, but Barbara was a little angel and didn't cry, even when the priest poured water over her head. She just fidgeted a bit as if to say, "Oh, that's cold! Let me see if I can get out of the way."

Beth went to church whenever she could. She didn't drive, so Donald had to take her. She didn't like being dependent on him to get around and decided it was time she got behind the wheel herself. She worked up her nerve and, heart pounding, told Donald she planned to get her driver's license.

"How will you do that?" he asked.

"I'll practice in the car. You can take me."

"Humph." He shook the newspaper he was reading. "Women drivers," he grumbled, barely audibly.

Beth was surprised when Donald himself initiated her driving lessons. He was not a patient teacher, so it was a good thing that Beth was a quick study. She passed her written test and got her permit, and the lessons commenced. Beth found the coordination of the clutch and the gas confusing at first. Don's impatience made her perspire, but she stuck with it. Four weeks after she'd gotten her permit, Beth was the proud owner of a New Jersey driver's license.

The following Sunday, Beth wanted to go to church, but Donald refused to take her. By this time, Beth had faced down a few obstacles in her life that might once have made her turn and run. This day, however, she plucked up her courage and drove herself and Barbara to St. Rose Church, about four miles away. Driving the car alone with baby Barbara made her stomach clench, but it was also exhilarating. Beth's heart sang as she cruised down Belmar Boulevard.

Holding the baby, Beth entered the chapel and genuflected. She turned right and went up the side aisle to the rows of votive candles in their red glass holders. Numerous tiny flames flickered, each signifying an individual prayer. Beth picked up a wooden match, touched it to a flame in one of the lit candles, then lit her own.

From her heart arose a prayer that was also a sorrow, a hope, and a dream. Beth let her worries lift, heaven-sent, along with her hopes and dreams for her own child. *Give me strength, Lord,* she prayed. *Give me courage.*

Beth threw herself into her new roles as wife, mother, and homeowner. She had longed for a home of her own; now she had one. Her husband had built it for her. Rolling that thought around in her mind gave her a sense of pleasant fullness in her heart. She'd sometimes say her new name out loud: "Mrs. Hoffman. Beth Hoffman." Or she'd say, "my husband."

Beth kept their home scrubbed and clean. She sewed curtains for the windows: red-and-white gingham check for the kitchen. They complemented the black-and-white tiled floor and the white wooden cabinets. A playful pattern for Barbara's room. Gold curtains for the dining room and gold, floor-length drapes for the living room to set off the neutral beige carpet and brown sofa. Don, who was an excellent carpenter, built a round coffee table for the L-shaped sofa and a four-foot bookshelf that took up an entire wall.

Beth set out to fill the bookshelf with books for Barbara and for herself. She learned how to cook—simple recipes at first. Then she built her repertoire. She could always tell which dishes were successes and which were failures. If he liked them, Don would clean his plate. If not, he'd complain. Beth was studious of her husband's happiness and was guided by his approval.

Once Beth had cleaned and furnished their home as well as she could on their meager budget, she turned her attention to the yard and garden. She planted a couple of blue hydrangea bushes at each of the house's front corners. When they did well, she added two small dogwood trees, one on either side of the front sidewalk. Over time, Beth added several fruit trees and a row of rosebushes along the driveway. She discovered she had a green thumb, and that yard work gave her a sense of peace and well-being. She'd bring Barbara outside with her, first in her bassinet then in a playpen.

Raising a child and making a home caused time to pass quickly. When Barbara was five, Beth and Donald added Donald, Jr. to the family. They called him Donnie.

Donald was puffed up with pride about having produced a male heir, but he took no part in changing diapers or burping the baby. That was all women's work.

Beth had known no life other than that of her chaotic childhood. She was happier now than she'd been as a little girl although she sometimes longed for the brief joys of her days on the cheerleading squad and as a writer for the high school newspaper. But she felt grateful to have her own home, for a husband who went to work every day, and for her beautiful children. Her heart sang every morning when she saw her children growing and healthy, and when she surveyed her home and the plants that were thriving under her care.

Beth had asked Don to get her a sewing machine. He'd found a secondhand Singer and she'd put it to good use. With her foot operating the pedal, she made it hum for hours as she made all of her own and the children's clothing. Feeding the soft cloth through the machine and listening to the children playing, she smiled to herself. Sewing was another of her discovered talents, and it had a meditative quality. If Beth didn't have everything she craved, she had enough. Pedaling away at the Singer, Beth made durable, everyday clothing and special outfits for Christmas and Easter.

Only Don had store-bought pants and shirts. He preferred them. Though Beth felt rebuffed, she told herself he needed to present a more polished appearance since he had to go out to work. She contented herself with caring for her home and her family. Every morning, she prayed her rosary, beseeching God for a good life for Barbara and baby Donnie. She prayed, too, for her mother and her siblings, especially Luke and Prissy.

But it seemed God wasn't listening. Either that or he thought Beth's prayers were as worthless as she often felt. In January 1954, when Beth was 22 years old and Prissy was 12, bad news arrived from Michigan—Priscilla had been killed in a car crash. She'd been out on an errand with Ada's friend when a dump truck ran a stop sign. Both Priscilla and Ada's friend were killed on impact.

The loss threw a shadow on Beth's soul—she'd failed to protect her baby sister. Beth didn't ask herself how that had become her job. The adults in Beth's life hadn't taken responsibility for much. Her father had blamed her and her siblings for a cold dinner, for no dinner, for their mother being absent, for the sky being blue. Ada had abandoned much of her responsibility to the family, and Beth had picked up as much as she could as a young child. Responsibility was something she simply accepted along with the guilt and burden that came with it.

Two years later, Beth gave birth to Ellery Ann. She was a tiny baby, only 17 inches long. She easily fit into the crook of Beth's arm as Beth cooked dinner or did chores. Looking into her daughter's tiny face, Beth's heart filled with love.

Donald had put an addition on the house to accommodate his growing family. They now had three bedrooms, a living room, dining room, an entry hall, and a full basement, with a tool shop and laundry area. They bought a used, 1950, meadow-green Ford pickup truck for Donald to drive to and from the trucking company where he worked. That left the family car, a 1948 Ford coupe, for Beth to drive to the grocery store and church.

Beth used her newfound freedom to create some family traditions. Fridays were ice cream night. After dinner, the kids got a bowl each and could add whatever toppings they chose: banana, peanuts, chocolate syrup, or sprinkles. Or everything at once. For birthdays, Beth would cook the birthday boy or girl's favorite meal and bake their favorite cake. Barbara liked steak for dinner and chocolate cake for dessert; Donnie wanted spaghetti and meatballs with lemon cake and lemon icing. Ellery was still too young to have a preference, while Don wanted lemon meringue pie served at his birthday celebration.

Meanwhile, Beth's fruit trees had grown to include a Queen Anne cherry tree, a peach tree, and a pear tree. They produced delicious fruits, which Beth used to make cherry pie and a variety of jams and jellies. Beth had hung birdfeeders in the trees and at the front-room window. Seeing the winged creatures visiting gladdened her heart, and the children delighted in them as well. They learned to identify blue jays, cardinals, robins, downy woodpeckers, goldfinches, sparrows, house finches, crows, and nuthatches.

Beth's life was full except for the companionship of her husband, whom she tried hard to make happy. Donald, however, remained elusive. His heart was simply not in it. He was disgruntled and restless and had maintained his practice of going out on a four-hour jaunt to get cigarettes or going fishing but never bringing home a fish.

Donald hurt Beth deeply with his philandering—oh, yes, she knew what he was doing when he left home on his regular nights out. Or at least, she suspected. On Sundays, he'd go to his boss's house to collect his pay. His boss, Robert Kennedy, played cards with a group of friends on Sunday nights. Robert wouldn't be home, and Donald would stay to watch a movie with Robert's wife, Lily. He'd finally come home around 11 o'clock. He wouldn't stay home to watch a movie with his own family, but he'd do it with Lily. Other nights he'd go tomcatting around by himself or with a neighbor, who took Donald to his hometown of Palisades Park to pick up women.

In time, Beth found out the hard way that what she'd always suspected was true. Her husband had brought her several unwanted gifts over the years: a variety of sexually transmitted diseases, including genital warts. The first time she had itching and burning in her genital area, followed by a yellow discharge, Beth was worried. Embarrassed, thinking she had someone gotten a vaginal infection, she spoke to Don about it.

"Call Dr. Sayers," he said.

Never in a million years would she have expected Dr. Sayers to tell her she had gonorrhea and genital warts. She gaped at him wordlessly. He merely went quietly about the business of giving her a prescription and telling her gently it might be wise to use a condom when she had intercourse, even with her husband.

This was tantamount to divulging that Don had been there before her. Beth was humiliated that she had to be treated by Dr. Sayers, their kindly family physician.

One night, when Donald, his brother Ryan, and the neighbor were in Donald's workshop in the basement, they added insult to injury. The men sometimes gathered there to do some work or see what Donald was up to. Mostly, though, they would gossip and drink beer.

Beth was reading quietly in the living room, right above Donald's workshop. The men became boisterous, and Beth couldn't help overhearing part of the conversation.

"I caught her ass," Donald said, laughing.

"You mean her ass caught you!" yelled the neighbor, Matt Novak.

Loud laughter erupted.

"Too bad she gave you the clap," he added.

"Dr. Sayers took care of that," said Ryan.

Anger burned inside Beth. Her own husband, the father of her children, was *laughing* about cavorting with other women and contracting a venereal disease. He was humiliating her in front of his brother and the neighbor.

Not only that. Beth had discovered that Donald had been telling his family that she drank. Beth! Who was virtually a teetotaler. Apparently, his family believed it. Why shouldn't they? They didn't see her on a daily basis. They had only his word to go on. Even if she were to deny it, blood is thicker than water. They'd cling to their beliefs about her and blame her for anything that went wrong.

Listening to these men—her husband, her brother-in-law, her neighbor—laughing at her pain, laughing at the disrespect her husband was showing her, Beth's heart hardened. Unable to move, she could only listen to their perverse conversation. It sent ice through her veins.

Her gaze fell upon the row of rose bushes she'd planted along the picket fence lining their long driveway.

Red, red roses, symbolizing love, beauty, and passion. None of which, she realized, she had. They were meant to celebrate her home, her new life, her growing family, but Beth felt only the prick of the thorns along their stem, the thorns in her side that might forever be lodged there, causing her to shed blood and tears.

Someday I will leave him, Beth thought. *Someday.*

Chapter: Twelve

A few months before Ellery Ann turned four, Beth had been feeling unwell and her period had become erratic. *I'm too young for the changes*, she thought. *I'm only 28.*

A visit to the doctor brought frightening news: Beth had a tumor.

Oh my God, what will happen to my kids if I die? I can't die. Donald will never take care of them properly. He'd just marry one of his trollops and she'd be as evil to my kids as Edith was to me. She shuddered at the thought.

Early one June morning, before anyone was up, Beth was sitting quietly, saying her rosary. As her fingers moved from decade to decade, she prayed…

"Hail Mary, full of grace…

"Our Father, who art in heaven…"

Her fingers fumbled and her thoughts scattered. *Please, God, please, help me. Don't take me from my children. Heal me. Save me.*

Gripping the prayer beads so tightly that her fingers turned white, Beth opened her eyes and saw—rosebuds. Her rosebushes had survived the long, cold, snowy winter. Not only had they survived, but they were thriving. Amongst the green leaves were red buds. Many, many rosebuds. There was her answer: the promise of a future, of beauty and love. As she sat perfectly still, drinking in this sight, Beth felt a quickening within. Her eyes flew open, and she knew: *I don't have a tumor. I'm pregnant.*

At St. Rose Church that Sunday, she lit a candle of thanks; her prayers had been answered—Doctor Sayers had confirmed the pregnancy. She was due in January. As St. Augustine had proclaimed, the sacraments of the church were "the visible form of an invisible grace." Beth had been rewarded with "an invisible grace" in the loveliest of ways: a renewed appreciation for her own life and the gift of a new one.

Chapter: Thirteen

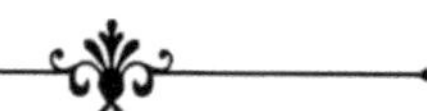

Snow began falling on the night of January 27, 1961. The rate of snowfall increased steadily, and the wind began howling around the eaves. The weatherman had forecast a blizzard.

Beth was tired. It had been a long day and her pregnancy was in full bloom. Her back had been twinging on and off all day. After she cleaned up the dinner dishes and got the kids settled, she was finally able to sit down. No sooner had she put her feet up than she felt the first contraction. It was strong. She looked down at her abdomen and she could see the whole thing tighten up as if there was a living creature inside.

Well, of course there's a living creature inside, Beth thought. *And he or she's on their way out.*

Her labor progressed quickly, and Beth called the doctor's office only to discover Dr. Sayers was out of town. The covering doctor would meet her at the hospital. Be advised, he warned, that the roads were slick. If she and her husband needed assistance, they should call the New Jersey State Troopers. Beth's stomach dropped.

Donald was silent, as usual, as he picked up her suitcase. Barbara, now 12 years old, stayed with the younger kids while Donald drove Beth to Fitkin Hospital.

Wall Township was quite rural in those days. The local hospital was only three miles away, but those were three miles through forest and sporadic residential clusters. Although the road was paved, it was covered in three feet of snow. The howling wind drove the snow so forcefully that visibility was near zero. The journey, in a word, was treacherous.

Donald's Ford pickup was sliding all over Gully Road as he navigated the crests and dips for which the road had been named. Donald peered intently over the steering wheel as Beth hung on for dear life. She didn't want to cry out, so she made great efforts to bite her tongue. She didn't want Donald angrier than he already was. Angry at life, it seemed. She knew her husband was moody and taciturn by nature, yet Beth longed for a kind word, for gentle reassurance. They were husband and wife. They had created another child together. That should be worth something. Tears pricked her eyes. Here she was, about to deliver their fourth child. The other three were healthy at home. They weren't wealthy, but they had a roof over their heads, and they had enough to eat. Their family should've been a happy one.

But no words were exchanged. Donald drove up to the hospital's front entrance and dropped Beth off. He barely gave her a peck on the cheek. Beth's heart ached with a familiar pain. It had been with her as long as she could remember, but she didn't really want to leave Don. Things weren't as bad as they'd been in her childhood. The imminent arrival of the new baby gave her hope. *Maybe*, she thought as she went in alone, *this child will reach his heart.*

An orderly wheeled Beth inside and placed her in the waiting room. The smell of antiseptic turned her stomach. Few of the chairs were filled. People tried to avoid driving on the treacherous roads. One woman stared vacantly into space. A child keened on his mother's lap, his arm obviously broken. An old man moaned in the corner next to an old woman, who held his hand.

Contractions gripped Beth's belly every five minutes. She squeezed her eyes shut and clutched the chair handles, trying to breathe through each contraction. She simply rested in between.

It was during one of these resting moments that the triage nurse called Beth's name. She lifted her head and called out, "Here!" The nurse scrambled around the edge of her cubicle to wheel Beth over to her desk and get her registered.

Luckily for Beth, the triage nurse was skilled and swift. Beth was soon escorted to the maternity wing and prepped for birth: hospital gown, enema, feet in cold stirrups.

Dr. Sayers' replacement was late, so Beth spent much of the time in her room alone. The nurses checked on her regularly, both before and after the new doctor's arrival in the wee hours of the morning.

After seven hours of intense labor, Beth and Don's new daughter was born early in the morning of January 28th. Beth wanted to name her Janet, which meant *gift of God.*

When Don came to visit, he smiled as he held his new baby girl.

She is *a gift*, Beth realized. *From tumor to bundle of joy.*

Beth's eyes softened as she gazed at the little baby trying to stuff her tiny fist into her mouth. *Yes, baby, I will lay down my life for you. Someday I'm going to get an education and a decent job. Then I can help provide for you.*

For the rest of that winter, Beth began to think she might have to lay down her life sooner than she'd expected. First, Barbara came home from school with chicken pox. She was miserable, lying in her bed with a fever and covered with itchy, red blisters. Beth organized an oatmeal bath schedule for Barbara and was in and out of her room applying calamine lotion all day long.

No sooner did her pox start to heal up than Donnie started scratching. Once again, Beth administered oatmeal baths and calamine lotion. She was run off her feet taking care of two ill children, the 4-year-old and the baby, while doing all the usual chores and cooking. The month flew by.

At the beginning of March, Donnie's blisters were finally healing up, and Beth was ready to resume normal life. As she looked down longingly at the living room couch, Ellery came running in.

"Mommy, mommy," she called. "Mommy, look! I look like Donnie." Ellery was holding out her arm where a few red spots had begun to swell.

Oh, no, not Ellery, too!

Indeed, Ellery, too. And then the baby, two weeks later. Beth had no adult company and, more importantly, no adult help. They had no electric dryer and no diaper service. She had to wash all the clothing and hang it out on the line even if it froze. In inclement weather, she strung a clothesline in the basement. Beth worried about the children getting scars from chicken pox, and Janet was so little, Beth couldn't soothe her with words. She just squirmed and cried.

Through it all, Beth remembered her vow: *Greater love hath no man…* She remembered her own childhood and how dreary and frightening it had been. She would give these children something better. But to do that, she needed a partner, a man to be the father.

She tried to talk with Donald about this. She wanted him to take part in family life. She asked him to spend more time at home with her and the children. But she met with an impenetrable wall. She was "nagging." What an easy out! No woman wanted to be a nag.

But I don't want to be his second choice, either, she thought.

Ironically, Donald always accused Beth of cheating. He seemed to think the saying "The best defense is a good offense" applied to infidelity. Consciously or unconsciously, that's what he was doing—defending himself by attributing his own salacious behavior to her. Knowing that, though, didn't make it any better.

Still, Beth stayed. She was determined to provide her children with a better upbringing than she'd had.

Her marriage to Don was not perfect, but it was better than her parents' relationship. She rationalized that she was laying her life down for her children, that this sacrifice of hers would give the children the benefit of an unbroken home and the presence of both a mother and father.

Beneath the surface of Beth's psyche, however, lurked another less lucid reason: She had the distinct but unarticulated belief that the tumult in her parents' marriage had been her fault. That she, a mere child, had somehow been the catalyst for their unhappiness, for her father's drinking. After all, she'd been the ugly duckling with big feet. It must be her fault, she believed deep down. Somehow, she was flawed and she'd brought this on herself. She'd made her bed; she had to sleep in it.

Not everything was such a trial. The children were a real joy. As they grew and changed and mastered new skills, Beth marveled at how wonderful, and how unique, they each were.

Barbara was precocious and outgoing. She excelled in school, especially in language and the arts. She was fearless and articulate, traits that drove her father crazy at the dinner table. He liked quiet and wanted to eat in peace. Throughout her teens, nighttime would find Barbara pounding away on her typewriter.

Donnie was also intelligent but showed it in different ways. He was Barbara's opposite. While she was verbose, he was the Sphinx. He rarely spoke but would communicate with expressions and grunts. He was a sensitive child and grew into a sensitive young man. His artwork was impressive, and his hands could work magic with all things mechanical: clocks, appliances, cars.

Ellery was cute as a button. Beth was sure she would become a housewife and mother. As a little girl, Ellery liked to carry a purse and take care of her baby dolls. She was a shy homebody. As she grew, she displayed a talent for organization, business, knitting, and sewing. But not cooking! Ellery liked to eat, but she was not gifted in the kitchen.

Ellery left the cooking to Janet. As a little girl, Janet loved her Betty Crocker Easy Bake Oven. She'd bake little cakes and frost them and give them as delicious snacks to the family. At 2 ½ years old, she was already a self-taught reader, sounding out words on cereal boxes during breakfast. Beth found this almost eerie, but it was simply a precursor of a natural academic excellence and love of languages.

As Barbara grew into her late teens, she became a real beauty—and a real challenge. Barbara had smooth, golden-brown hair, an aquiline nose, and green eyes. She spoke French and taught it to Janet. In fact, she was like a second mother to her youngest sister. When Janet was a baby, Barbara would change Janet's diapers. Later, when Barbara started dating, she taught Janet how to wait for the man to come around and open her car door for her. Janet was enthralled with her beautiful, intelligent older sister.

It was the mid-'60s, the Beatles were singing "I Wanna Hold Your Hand," and the girls were wearing long tresses and go-go boots. More compelling than Twiggy and prettier than Eric Clapton's muse (Pattie Boyd), Barbara looked like a model. When she mimicked the latest fashions and started wearing tight sweaters and makeup, Donald blew his top. There were tears, shouting, and slammed doors.

When Barbara felt her creativity rise in the middle of the night, the clackety-clack of her typewriter keys woke Donald from a sound sleep. He was livid and told her in no uncertain terms that she could write her stories during the daytime. She told him he was a grump and that he was stifling her inspiration.

Barbara's frustration motivated her to write in secret to her grandmother, Ada, who had remarried, was now Mrs. Kinsinger and lived in California. After Barbara graduated from high school, she informed Beth and Don that she was going to live with Grandma Kinsinger in San Bernardino.

A few weeks later, Donald, Beth, and the children stood behind a chain-link fence and watched her plane lift off from the runway at Newark Airport. Although no one knew it at the time, Barbara would never return. Even so, Janet was so devastated that they had to pry her hands off the fence that separated the stunned family from the runway.

The departure of the eldest daughter did nothing to help the desperate family situation, so Beth decided she'd better save some money for a rainy day. The day she told Donald she'd gotten a job, all hell broke loose. It was the longest "conversation" she'd had with Donald in a long time.

"What do you mean, you got a job? Who said you could get a job?"

Although her gut was clenching, Beth kept her voice low and even. "The extra money I bring home will help. The children are getting older. They don't need me as much, and you'll be here when I'm away."

Donald was fuming. He didn't want to be tied down at home after years of roaming free in the evening. "No wife of mine is going out to work, especially not at night!" Donald was pacing through the living and dining room in his white tee shirt and work pants.

Beth sat calmly on the couch, her hands folded in her lap. "It's not at night. I'll be hostessing at Le Deauville Inn in the evenings. I will be home at night."

"Don't argue with me, Beth! I said it and that's it."

"I'm not arguing, but I am going out to work." She looked sideways at him. "*You* go out at night, and it's not to work. How is that any better?"

The argument carried on until Donald, frustrated, angry, and looking for an excuse, grabbed his keys and roared out of the driveway in his pickup truck, spewing her roses with gravel and exhaust as he left.

Beth went to work, but that didn't mean Donald stayed home in the evenings. Beth would cook supper before she left. Donald sat with the children and wolfed it down in silence. Well, all but his angry mastication. Then he'd shower, dress, and leave without telling the children where he was going.

Sometimes he'd pursue women, as he'd always done, but this new attitude of Beth's got under his skin. *Who does she think she is? She must be cheating on me, goddamn it.* He began to spy on her at work.

Beth's workplace, Le Deauville Inn, was an English country mansion that had several beautiful dining rooms, an elegant bar, a lovely patio, and lush, expansive grounds. Built in 1925, it was famous for its French cuisine, sophisticated dining, and superb service.

Beth was a stylish addition to the inn. Lovely and graceful by nature, Beth quickly learned the names of all the regular patrons. She knew the names of their children and grandchildren, and their seating and drink preferences as well. The men especially enjoyed seeing her warm smile and sparkling eyes, but Beth was careful to be deferential to the wives so as not to seem a threat.

In direct contrast to all this gentility, Donald would drive over in the evenings and stalk around the mansion, watching for signs of infidelity. He let his imagination run so wild that he thought Beth was having a tryst in the upstairs powder room.

There was a convenient tree outside the powder room, and Donald decided to scale it so he could get a better view. Sure enough, Beth came up and closed herself in.

"Uh, huh. Just as I thought," Donald muttered to himself as he shifted in the branches to get a closer look. "She's waiting for her lover."

He was disappointed when Beth lifted her dress, did her business, washed her hands, and departed.

Grumbling and certain he would strike pay dirt if he stayed, Donald remained in the tree for three more hours. He climbed down, stiff and cold, but would not admit he was wrong.

Arguments between Donald and Beth became more frequent. Ten-year-old Janet heard the angry tone but didn't understand why they were fighting. She would hide in her bed and pull the covers over her head, fearful of what might happen. Fifteen-year-old Ellery turned up the radio in her room to drown out these battles, and 17-year-old Donnie simply left in his 1965 Ford Fairlane. His father would often follow, seeking solace elsewhere. Had he sought it at home, he would have gotten it, but for him the grass was always greener on the other side of the fence.

Beth would embrace the calm in the wake of the storm, and she would dream. She dreamt of returning to school, first to earn her high school diploma and then going on to become a nurse. Laying down her life for her children as well as those who needed healing would be another way to contribute to society, to fulfill her purpose in life.

"Please, God," she prayed, "help me to be strong, to love my children, and to make the right decisions."

I can be a role model for the kids, she thought. *I'm an example no matter what I do. This is no kind of life for them. I want them to have something better.*

Chapter: Fourteen

For a few weeks now, Beth had noticed itching in her genital area and burning while she urinated. When it grew worse and she detected a yellow discharge, she scheduled a doctor's appointment. She already knew what it was: more proof of Don's adultery.

But STDs weren't the only proof of Donald's dalliances. Donald's brother George and his wife, Emily, descended upon the house one evening when Donald was out. That was a surprise in itself since no one in Donald's family was comfortable with drop-in visits.

When the knock came on the back door, Beth was startled. Although night had yet to fall, dusk had settled, and Donald wasn't home. She went to the door with some trepidation. There had been stalkers in the neighborhood, and one night Beth had looked up to see a man staring at her through the window. By the time the police arrived, he'd long since disappeared. But tonight, when Beth went to the door, there stood George and Emily. Their faces were grim, and they stepped inside when Beth held the door. They wasted no time relating what had happened that evening.

Apparently, Donald had been dating one particular woman, Jane Elizabeth, regularly. She'd been the first wife of Donald's employer, Robert Kennedy. It was so absurd that Beth felt a wholly inappropriate bubble of laughter rising in her chest. She fought it back. *I guess Robert and Donald have similar tastes,* she thought, *and Donald doesn't mind taking up with Robert's castoffs.*

Once her initial reaction receded, she felt sick to her stomach.

George and Emily exchanged a look that seemed to settle the responsibility of the telling. Emily was a notorious gossip, so the task wasn't such a burden.

"We thought you should know," said Emily, snapping her gum. "Donald was up at our place about half an hour ago."

"Ok."

"He was in a terrible state. Said he wanted to marry Jane Elizabeth, but she wouldn't have him."

Beth felt ice shoot through her veins. Her mind struggled to close itself off from this tale. She did not want to hear it.

"We thought you should know. He has a gun."

Beth's eyes widened and her mouth fell open, but she remained silent.

"He was cryin' and wailin' about it. Said he was gonna shoot hisself."

Beth's stomach dropped.

"We told 'im to go home," Charlie busted in. "He's not gonna shoot himself, otherwise he never woulda told us. But we took the gun away from him anyway."

So, there it was, out on the table. Now everyone would know if they didn't already. The whole family, the whole town. Her children's friends would tell her children. She'd be a laughingstock. Not that she cared much about that. *How would the children take it?*

This was really the end. For years, Beth had put up with Donald's absences, his moods, his morose insistence that no one talk at the dinner table. She'd even put up with his tomcatting around town, first by himself then with their neighbor Matt Novak. These men were no better than her father.

Maybe they're worse, she thought. *At least my father had an illness. He was an alcoholic*. When he wasn't drinking, he was a good person, a smart and funny man, a hard worker. But these men—her own husband—did these things stone-cold sober.

Beth had to admit some hard truths. She was sad and lonely. She had poured her heart into this home and this family. Her family. Her children. Donald's children. She had made the holidays special. She'd baked homemade cookies at Christmas, and she and the children had decorated them. They'd cut out shapes from the sugar-cookie dough then paint them with colored icing. They would roll out the gingerbread dough and cut out the gingerbread men.

Why are there no gingerbread women? she wondered. *Because it's a man's world. Men always get their own way.*

She'd poured herself into her family and home. *And for what? For Donald to go off and try to marry someone else while he's still married to me!*

This moment had been sneaking up on her, she knew. When Donnie had turned 14, he'd complained to his father, "I don't wanna go to church anymore." When Donald agreed and gave him permission to stop attending church, the other kids jumped ship also. Beth felt lost.

That had all been undermining enough. In the face of this open infidelity, though, she was stunned. *Nothing I do is turning out right,* she thought. *I need to get away from him. He never really wanted to be married to me.*

She could see that now. *For years, he hasn't wanted anything to do with me or the children. He always goes somewhere else in the evening. He's been having affairs with women all our married life. Now he's trying to marry someone else behind my back. That's it. I'm done.*

Chapter: Fifteen

The next night, Beth quietly served dinner as usual. Donald liked his meals simple, so tonight it was pork chops, mashed potatoes, and peas. Beth set his plate in front of him first then handed each of the children their servings.

The meal passed in silence.

Beth knew what was coming. He would dress and leave, so she had to do this before he was gone.

When Donald finished his shower and came into the bedroom to dress, she was waiting.

“I’d like to talk with you.”

“I’m going out.”

“That’s actually what it’s about.”

“Oh, now you’re gonna nag me again. It’s okay for you to go out at night, but not for me? Well, I’m going.”

"I don't go 'out' at night. I go to a job, where I work, and I'm paid."

"Paid to do what, I wonder."

Beth steeled herself against the insulting innuendo. "We need to talk about your 'going out.' You've been going out at night our whole married life. It's time you stayed home and spent some time with me and the children."

"Beth, I work all day to put food on the table and a roof over your head." He was fully dressed now and pulled a comb through his short, curly, dark hair as he stood in front of the mirror. "I'm going out for a pack of cigarettes. So don't nag me about it."

"Since when does it take four hours to get a pack of cigarettes? You could walk to the store and back in ten minutes."

Without another word, Donald reached for his jacket and stepped toward the bedroom door.

"Donald, I mean it. I've had enough. The children deserve more. You need to stop going out with Matt. You need to stop him from insulting the children, especially Ellery. He calls her Porky Pig! You shouldn't let him speak like that to her."

"He's just teasing."

"It's not teasing, but that's not the worst of it. You need to stop seeing other women."

Donald whipped his head around and fixed her with a sharp look.

"I mean it. You have to choose. You either stop going out with him and seeing other women or I'm leaving. If you're not going to stop, I don't want anything to do with you."

In a flash, Donald stepped so close to her Beth could feel his hot breath on her face.

"You don't give me ultimatums. I'm the man of this family, and I'll do what I want. If you want to leave, that's up to you. I'll have someone in here to replace you so fast, your head will spin. And the children will stay with me."

"Over my dead body."

He turned to go.

Chapter: Sixteen

One afternoon a few weeks later, Beth was folding clothing when Janet came in from school. After Janet got settled, Beth called to her.

Janet glanced out the window as she entered the dining room. Their 15-foot peach tree was split down the center. It looked as if a giant had split it with an axe. "What happened to the peach tree?" she asked.

"Lightning struck it during the night."

Janet sat down next to her black-and-white cat, Spooky, who was lying on the floor, and began scratching under his chin and behind his ears. He began to purr, a comforting rumble.

"I have something to tell you," Beth said. "Your father and I are getting a divorce."

Janet had never heard the "D-word" before, at least not in casual conversation. Janet's vision narrowed suddenly into a black tunnel. She no longer felt Spooky's fur or heard his rumbling purr. Just like that, her world cracked right open, like Humpty Dumpty. Like the peach tree in the backyard. Everything just cracked wide open. And would never be the same. Not ever, ever again.

Chapter: Seventeen

The house on 17th Avenue in West Bank left a lot to be desired. A single narrow story, it had only one bedroom. It was a tiny home. The hallway was painted like an American flag: red and white stripes on the right, blue with white stars on the left. The trapdoor to the Yankee cellar was smack in the middle of the entrance to the eat-in kitchen.

The neighborhood was rough and rundown, but that was all Beth could afford. She'd purchased the place with her share of the Belmar Boulevard home. Donnie had stayed with his father, so it would be a little easier to make this work with the girls. She bought a pull-out couch, where she slept at night. It wasn't ideal, but at least she was able to stay in the same school district. That was important to her. She was trying to minimize the changes to Ellery's and Janet's lives.

Through it all, Beth worried about the children. There was plenty to worry about. Barbara, who was three thousand miles away, was angry and didn't welcome input from her mother. Donnie, her quiet, sensitive son, was now constantly exposed to his father's lifestyle and its influences with no one and nothing to act as a buffer. And her girls ... her girls were now living in poverty.

If only I'd chosen more carefully, she thought, after the girls were asleep, on the first night in their new home. *If only I could have made things work.*

But what could she have done? She had been raised by a father who was constantly drunk and violent. Her mother hadn't been much better. Her husband thought so little of her that he hid their marriage and her pregnancy from his family until it could no longer be avoided. He hadn't honored her or his vows. He'd ruined her name by lying to his family about her, saying she drank the way her father had and that she had slept with other men.

These thoughts went around and around in Beth's head. She couldn't think straight. Out of desperation, she fell to her knees and put her forehead on the couch. "Help me, God. I've made such a mess of things. Why doesn't anyone love me? My father didn't. My mother—my own mother—didn't. My husband didn't, even after I gave myself to him in the most intimate and special way possible. Please, please help me now."

Wearily, Beth looked up and saw something she'd missed earlier. Her new home had a huge American flag painted all the way down the hall. The flag of the United States of America. It symbolized the land of the free and the home of the brave.

Beth, she thought, *that's who you are. No more suppressing your feelings. No need to overlook disrespect, adultery, and mocking laughter. You. Are. Free.*

She had released herself from her cage.

Beth showed her courage during the days and nights that followed. She worked hard to make ends meet, taking on three jobs. During the day, she put in a full shift at Sonetronics, right down the street, wiring AM/FM radios on an assembly line. At night she hostessed at Le Deauville Inn, and she cleaned houses on the weekends.

Unfortunately, she was rarely home. That meant little rest for her, and no supervision for Janet. Ellery now had her driver's license and drove a 1972 vermillion Ford Pinto. Given her new mobility, Ellery was frequently absent from home. That meant that 12-year-old Janet was often left alone.

Beth and the girls had moved to 17th Avenue, directly across from the West Bank Elementary School, during the summer. When school started up again in September, Ellery drove herself to the high school and Janet took the bus to the middle school. On the first day, Janet dressed carefully in a floral skirt and top that Beth had sewn. She completed the outfit with a pair of new high-heels.

Janet had dressed up for the first day of school every year since kindergarten. It showed her enthusiasm and respect. At least it had in her previous neighborhood. At this West Bank bus stop, everyone else was dressed casually in jeans. Talk about the odd man out. Not only did Janet stick out in this group—which one of these is not like the other?—but she was an intellectual child, curious and shy.

As she sat on the steps in front of the white clapboard Methodist church, waiting for the bus, she saw a dark smudge on her new shoes. She licked her finger and cleaned it off. Other kids look at her askance and made quiet, disparaging comments. When the bus finally delivered them to school, the local boys followed her around that day and every other day, bumping into her and knocking her into her locker.

She bore this injustice for a long time, withdrawing further and further into herself. She tried ignoring them. She tried saying nothing, doing nothing. She hoped they would just stop. But they didn't stop; they got worse.

The boys knew where Janet lived, and they came to the house after school when no one else was home. Janet knew who was at the door, and she was afraid. She waited, sitting far away from the windows, trying to be invisible and hoping they would go away.

They didn't go away. Instead, they pushed through a basement window, climbed into the cellar, and tried to open the Yankee cellar door. Janet stood a kitchen chair on the door and hung back, clenching her fists, silently waiting. The boys pushed and pushed, all three of them—Larry Castor, Jeff Castor, and Steve Anderson. The door rose, quivering six inches above their combined power. Then it flopped back down. They pushed again. Janet remained seated, silent, and afraid. She didn't know that she could call the police. She was used to an atmosphere of silence and a lack of communication. She didn't know how to ask for help or how to talk about anything. She was frozen.

"Push," yelled one of them. "Harder."

The boys pushed again, together. Harder. The door rose higher, the chair wobbling. Janet could see the tops of their heads. Then it dropped back down. They couldn't lift it.

Janet was spared. For the time being.

Chapter: Eighteen

Barbara wasn't so lucky. After her adolescent fantasies of a loving grandmother who would nourish her every creative whim dissolved in the face of reality, Barbara decided to pack up and move to Los Angeles. Beautiful, talented, and determined, Barbara landed a job at a popular magazine. She worked her way up to editor by the age of 24. She traveled to Europe, stayed at youth hostels, and traversed countries by train. Men often eyed the young, mysterious beauty; some made offers. She would occasionally flirt with them, but she was cautious. One man was smoother and more charming than the others. He kept a low profile and was perfectly polite. He chatted with her about his business and home in London and asked whether he could write to her.

After two years of writing to one another and one visit each in LA and London, Niall proposed. Barbara was delighted to accept the proposal *and* the diamond ring. She gave up her job and moved to London.

Unfortunately, Niall didn't like Barbara's midnight creativity any more than her father had, but he had a much more violent way of showing it. At first, Barbara tried hard to please her husband. She wrote during the day while Niall was at work. She also began painting in watercolors and oils, and found some success through local galleries. She walked to the corner market every day for fresh meat or fish and vegetables. She felt very British with her woven basket, and she enjoyed meeting the local shopkeepers and neighbors. But Niall was picky. He called it "precise" and "discriminating," and Barbara learned not to argue over small disagreements.

One evening, Niall returned from work later than expected. Barbara had kept his dinner warm in the oven, but the chicken in white wine had grown dry. Barbara was more shocked that he backhanded her than that one of her teeth burst out of her mouth and skittered across the kitchen floor.

Niall remained cool in the face of Barbara's upset. He gave her a perfunctory apology but turned the conversation to office matters. He patted the chair next to him, indicating he wanted her to sit and keep him company while he ate his dinner. He carried on as if nothing out of the ordinary had happened.

Barbara was numb. After washing up, she tried to talk to Niall.

"Oh, Pet," he said, sitting next to her on the settee in their little London cottage, "I am sorry. I get very cranky sometimes. Let me get you some ice."

Barbara was mollified, but Niall's crankiness didn't improve. After three years, two black eyes, and a concussion, Barbara bought a one-way ticket back to LA. Resuming her life proved difficult, though. She had used up her savings to move first to London and then back to California. She had a three-year gap in her resume. She sought a higher salary than the graduates fresh out of college. She had a tough time breaking back into the publishing world. She now had a deficit, both financial and emotional, that she needed to make up.

The strain widened an existing crevice in Barbara's personality. She became convinced that her own mother had named her *Barbara* because it meant *stranger*. The idea was absurd, of course. When Beth had given birth to Barbara in 1948 at the tender age of 17 years and six weeks, she had no baby name book. She didn't go to the library to look up potential baby names. Beth had given her beloved baby daughter the name of the friend she treasured most.

But Barbara was deaf to any voice but her own. She began to write letters, diatribes really, blaming Beth for every slight and wrong that had been done to her (Barbara). Had she agreed to see a counselor or a psychiatrist, she would have been diagnosed with a personality disorder, but she refused to go. Nothing was wrong with her. It was everyone else who fell down on the job, who was rude or ignorant. Barbara knew what was wrong in each situation and knew how to fix everything—except her own life.

Chapter: Nineteen

Beth made two good friends at Le Deauville Inn. Gretchen was a real madame, a sixtyish woman with snow-white hair that was always drawn up in a bun. It looked as if she powdered her face *and* her hair. Michael was in his forties, Irish, and had a lilting brogue that gladdened the heart.

Gretchen and Michael had proved their worth as friends simply by encouraging and supporting Beth in her quest to break free from her cheating, neglectful husband and to get an education so she could provide for the children.

They also urged her to get out and meet people, to devote some time to play. This wasn't easy to do while working three jobs, but Beth trusted her friends and took their counsel to heart. She started by joining them at a local bar for cocktails one Friday night.

The bar was buzzing with noise and activity. The clink of bottles against glasses occurred with regularity, punctuated by laughter here and there. Beth felt awkward in this setting. Michael was a regular, so she followed him as he moved through the throng. Gretchen swept stalwartly behind her like a reliable battleship through the waves.

If Gretchen can do it, I can do it, Beth told herself.

Gretchen ordered a wine spritzer and Beth followed her lead.

"Ach, and what do ya call that, I ask? Sure, and you'll be wishing you ordered a Guinness," teased Michael. Guinness Stout was his drink.

The trio laughed and had to shout to hear each other above the din. During the evening, Beth saw men giving her the once-over.

Emboldened by the unfamiliar effects of the wine, Beth told her friends, "My divorce finally came through, so I guess it's okay that I'm out and about."

"It's about time," Gretchen gently scolded. "Donald certainly didn't wait for a divorce to get himself some extra company."

Michael shot her a look and patted Beth's hand. "There, there, darlin'. Steady on. You did nothing wrong and you're doing everything right."

"Speaking of doing everything right, I have some good news to share. I got into the Home Health Aide program."

Michael congratulated her.

Gretchen, true to her sometimes-acerbic nature, asked, “Are you sure that isn’t too much for you, working three jobs? How will you manage?”

“Oh, I’ll be giving up the Sonetronics job. This program has an on-the-job training section, and I qualified for that. So, I’ll get paid while I’m learning.”

As they were drinking a toast, a handsome man approached. He ignored Michael’s warning glance and asked Beth for a dance. When she declined, Gretchen butted in. “Oh, go on, Beth, relax and enjoy yourself. It’s only a dance.” She waved her hands at Beth in a shooing motion.

Embarrassed, Beth allowed the man to lead her onto the dance floor. Someone chose Percy Sledge’s “When a Man Loves a Woman” from the jukebox, and the man slid his arms around her, holding her close.

“Relax, baby,” said the man in her ear. “I’ve got you.” He settled his hand on her hips.

That’s what I’m worried about, she thought. She couldn’t decide whether it felt good or bad. *A little of both.*

When the song ended, Beth excused herself and went back to her friends. “Nothing like jumping in at the deep end,” she quipped. “Maybe I’m not ready for this yet.”

Later, at home, Beth reflected on the evening and her awkwardness. *It was just an invitation to dance*, she thought.

Oh, yeah? Then why did he push against me like that? asked her alter ego.

She felt squishy and uncomfortable inside.

Maybe I was sending out the wrong message, she thought, unconsciously wringing her hands. *Maybe I'm not meant to be in a relationship. Maybe there's something wrong with me.*

Feeling every inch a cuckolded wife and middle-aged mother, Beth bowed her head in misery.

Chapter: Twenty

A sharp rap on the door early the next morning startled Beth, causing her to slosh her coffee. She was home on a rare day off before she started her new training.

Beth went to the front door and opened it. There stood two angry men, one looking quite worse for the wear. It was Donald and his brother Ryan. Without a "good morning" or a "howdy do," Ryan marched Donald inside then turned to face her.

"In case you were wondering how Donald is, he's got cancer."

Beth was at a loss for words as her thoughts collided with one another. *What are they doing here? Donald looks terrible. They have no right to march into my home like this.*

Ryan put a suitcase on the floor. Straight-faced, he announced, "He's your husband. You gave him the cancer, so you can take care of him." And out he walked.

Beth just stared. *Is this really happening?* Even though she *knew* she hadn't given him cancer, a sense of shame washed over her, followed by a wave of anger. Hampered by her upbringing, however, she was unable to articulate this, even to herself.

Donald's clothes were hanging off of his gaunt frame. He was so weak, he had a hard time simply standing up. She felt a weight settle on her shoulders and in her chest. The light on the horizon turned dark as if storm clouds had just obscured the sun. She heard the sound of her freedom fizzling with an audible crackling at the edge of her consciousness.

I caused him cancer? she thought. *How? Maybe his late-night wanderings did that.* But she said nothing. At forty-three years old, her responses were too deeply ingrained.

Despite herself and the unjust situation, she felt a wave of pity and waved Donald to the lounge chair. "Would you like a cup of coffee?"

He nodded.

After setting his coffee next to him—three sugars and milk, as usual—she settled herself on the sofa.

"Donald, we have to talk about this. If you're going to stay here, we have to settle some things."

Donald refused to talk about the past. He wouldn't acknowledge his fault in the divorce. He remained as morose as ever, particularly with the gloom of his illness now hanging over him. After he changed out of his clothes and put on a thin, brown terrycloth robe, he never got dressed again.

Beth sheltered him, cooked for him, and did his laundry—all while she juggled her new position and two other jobs. She gave him the pullout sofa bed, where she usually slept, and bunked with the girls in their room. It was a tight squeeze.

When Gretchen and Michael found out that Ryan had dumped Don on Beth's doorstep, they went ballistic.

"Why on earth did you let them walk into your home?" Gretchen scolded. "You should've told them to take a hike."

"Beth, you don't owe him. If anything, he owes you," said Michael.

Listening to her friends, Beth felt even worse. Not only was her whole life disrupted again, she felt like a doormat. She had allowed her husband to walk all over her again.

The girls were freaked out by this whole situation. First, their lives had been disrupted by the divorce and the move to an unfriendly neighborhood. Next, their uncle angrily dumped their father on their doorstep, claiming their mother gave him cancer.

Cancer. Janet's mind drew a blank. Whether out of denial or ignorance, she didn't put two and two together. She didn't know that cancer usually meant death, but she knew something was radically wrong.

On the morning of January 6, 1974, Donald began breathing strangely—a thin, hollow, keening sound. It was such a frightening sound that Janet hid behind the door to the only bedroom.

Beth called an ambulance, and she and the girls followed it to Point Pleasant Hospital. As the two vehicles grew closer to the end of their journey, the radio in Beth's car played a new song by the Rolling Stones.

"Uh Aa-ngie, Aa-ngie," Mick Jagger sang, "where will it lead us from here?"

Beth's stomach was in knots as she drove. Even though Don had been a lousy husband, he was still the kids' father. He existed. Donnie lived with him although Beth doubted there'd been much father-son bonding. It gave some sort of psychological structure to their lives albeit a dysfunctional one. But now …

How can this be happening? What will happen to the kids now? It's all on me. Oh God, help me.

But Beth didn't have much time to worry. Donald was dead on arrival at the hospital. A few days later, Beth and Janet went to the funeral parlor a few hours early to make sure everything was ready for the viewing. The director walked in looking very friendly but came up behind Janet and grabbed the Levi's tag on the back pocket of her pants. Janet was numb with shock over everything that life had dumped on her in the past few months and said nothing. But what a creep! Grabbing a feel at her dead father's viewing.

A black limousine pulled up in front of their tiny home the next morning, the morning of the funeral. The contrast between its sleek elegance and their poverty made the day even more somber. Snow fell heavily as the limo shushed through the deserted streets toward the highway.

Whump! Whump! Two snowballs splatted on the windshield. The impact seemed to punch Beth in the chest. It felt like a violation in the enclosed world of their grief. Two pubescent boys stood boldly in a nearby field. They didn't even turn away or try to hide. No shame. Janet sank even further into her seat and herself.

Beth, Donnie, Ellery, and Janet sat in the front row at the funeral parlor. Barbara hadn't returned for her father's funeral. She remained angry and estranged from her mother, except when writing poison-pen letters that blamed Beth for everything wrong in Barbara's life. Don's former lover, Jane Elizabeth, hadn't dared to show her face. *That was just as well,* thought Beth. But Beth noticed when Lily Kennedy arrived. Lily represented Don's employer, so Beth motioned to Lily to come up and join the family. Lily just looked back and shook her hand.

Stung by this refusal, Beth flushed and turned around. Unfortunately, sound carried well inside the room, and she heard an exchange between two of the women in the back.

"Who's that?"

"The first one, that's his wife. The other one, Lily, that's his girlfriend."

Talk was just that: talk. What counted was action. Bearing. Dignity. Beth had that in spades, over and above the present company. During the service, she sat ramrod straight, in a simple but elegant black dress and heels, her children aligned with her. The backbiters might talk, but they admired her.

Chapter: Twenty-One

Beth stood 12 feet up on the ladder as she finished applying stain to the last of the cedar shingles. Climbing down, she admired her handiwork. She had a right to feel proud and pleased. After nursing then burying her ex-husband, she purchased a newer, bilevel home so she and the children could live in their old neighborhood. Beth had been able to swing the mortgage because of her position as a home health aide at Jersey Shore Medical Center. The house had enough bedrooms for all of them, including Donnie, and the old neighborhood was much nicer, much more genteel.

Beth was relieved that she could shelter *all* of her children—even Barbara, if she came home. After all, it wasn't just the girls who had felt the effects of their father's absence. Donnie had been impacted all his life by his father's neglect and had sought comfort among friends who drank and smoked pot regularly. Donnie enjoyed the high and bonded with his friends during activities that included getting wasted.

Beth was desperately trying to hold down multiple jobs while studying to get ahead. Jersey Shore was a teaching hospital, so it provided medical assistance to patients while teaching health-science students like doctors and nurses. Beth was excited to be in this atmosphere, surrounded by experienced health-care professionals. She learned at a rapid pace, was quick to put her new skills to use, and had good people skills. She was well-liked by doctors, nurses, and patients alike.

One day Beth was going from the cafeteria back to her floor when Dr. Grand stopped her in the hallway. Beth had first met Dr. Grand when she began her position as a health aide at the hospital. Watching her work, he'd recognized her intelligence and potential and had offered to serve as her mentor.

"Beth, I'm glad I caught you. You know that I think your work is exemplary. I believe you're interested in going to nursing school. Am I right about that?"

As Beth looked up at Dr. Grand—he was well over six feet tall—time seemed to slow down. The afternoon sun shone through the floor-to-ceiling hallway windows behind him, giving him an otherworldly glow. His smile reached all the way to his eyes, which crinkled around the edges. The message reached Beth subliminally: something good was about to happen.

After Beth assured him that he was correct, Dr. Grand told her that he would give her a written recommendation for admission into the nursing program. Beth was already on the waitlist, but with his recommendation, her name would go to the top. For the rest of the day, Beth's thoughts sparkled and spun about a foot above her head.

Soon enough, Beth found herself donning the white dress shoes of a nursing uniform. Her confidence grew with every test she aced and every positive comment she got. She still prayed every day, and when she was confronting a particularly difficult situation prayed constantly.

One such situation involved her clinical rotation at the local psychiatric hospital in Easton, New Jersey. Known simply as "Easton," the hospital complex was spread over about 500 acres. Beth had several patients on her caseload, including Harold.

Harold had been diagnosed with schizophrenia. During a hallucination, Harold had received word from Satan that his wife, a lovely woman named Clara, was a succubus—a demon in spirit form who copulates with sleeping men. Frightened, Harold had grabbed a butcher's knife from the kitchen, crept into the bathroom while the sound of the running water muffled his approach, and stabbed the demon repeatedly in the chest.

Harold got another fright when his wife, covered in blood, suddenly appeared in the demon's place. Gripped by panic and confused by the transformation, Harold called 9-1-1. Clara died of her wounds, and Harold was remanded to Easton. His hallucinations were kept under control by massive amounts of Haldol, except when he cheeked it. Then he could be a little bit … unpredictable.

Beth walked over to Harold's cottage, the brick building where he and other patients were housed, to check his vitals and do a general check-up. Harold was seated in a chair watching TV. As she bent over to listen to his heart rate, Harold fixed his gaze on her breasts. Although her skin began to crawl, Beth concentrated on her assessment—heart rate, temperature, blood pressure.

Folding her stethoscope into her pocket, Beth sat down opposite her patient. "How are you today, Harold? Your heart rate is a little high. Are you feeling anxious?"

Harold gazed back, wide-eyed. A line of drool ran down the side of his mouth.

"Would you like to take a walk with me down to the lake?" Beth asked.

Beth had seen the lake from a distance. From time to time, a pair of swans appeared there. She thought it might be just the right atmosphere to settle Harold's nerves.

"Sure, I'll take a short walk with you."

As they strolled over, Beth chatted with Harold, but he remained mute. Once they drew near to the lake, Harold turned, grabbed Beth, and planted his mouth on hers. She felt an unwelcome thrust against her leg.

Shit! she thought, pushing her arms up and out to break Harold's embrace. He dropped back, panting.

"Harold! That's inappropriate. You shouldn't grab me like that."

"What the hell?" he spouted. "You invited me to come to the lake with you."

"Yes, I invited you to walk with me to the lake, but I didn't invite you to kiss me or to do anything else."

"Yes, you did." Harold was growing agitated. "How stupid are you? That's what 'going to the lake' means. It means we're gonna do it."

Beth was both revolted and frightened, but she was careful not to show it.

"Well, now we're going to walk back, and while we do, you'll tell me what kind of thoughts you've been having lately and how you're getting along with the other residents of your cottage." *And I'll work on slowing my breathing and my own heart rate*, she thought. *And I won't have to learn this lesson twice.*

Chapter: Twenty-Two

The new home in which Beth and the children lived was only a block away from Janet's best friend, Frank DeGroot. Frank and Janet spent a lot of their free time walking and talking. They were creative and intelligent; they would walk for miles with ease and not even notice the time that had gone by.

While Beth was learning lessons on the job at Easton, Ellery had developed a relationship with Artie Gray, a young man from West Bank with criminal tendencies. Ellery had learned to comfort herself with food during the family's earlier, tumultuous years. As a result, she was a bit plump. She was also self-conscious, shy, and had little experience with the opposite sex.

A sharp character, Artie came sniffing after her like a hound dog. Ellery, who still suffered from low self-esteem after her childhood of neglect by her father and the verbal abuse of their neighbor Matt, basked in this attention.

Beth was trying hard to find time to spend with the kids, especially Ellery and Janet, but her jobs and schooling kept her away from home day and night. Hard as it was to squeeze in recreation time, Beth did manage to find an afternoon to take the girls shopping at the local mall. She drove the girls in her clunky, old, magenta-colored Chevy sedan. The paint had seen better days, and the finish was more buffed out than shiny. Ellery called the front seat, so Janet ended up in the back.

As they exited the freeway, Ellery screeched. "Oh, my god, there's a turtle in the road!"

Sure enough, a huge snapping turtle was lumbering across the exit ramp. At the rate he was going, he was sure to get squashed flat.

Ellery and Janet set up a protest. As young women, they were notorious for protecting the animals that came within their sphere, even to a level of absurdity.

"Don't run it over!" yelled Ellery.

"We have to save it!" Janet cried.

Ignoring the danger to her own life, Beth pulled to the side of the exit ramp, checked for oncoming traffic, and ran into the middle of the road. The turtle saw her coming and hissed, but she grabbed it with both hands and ran to a grassy area that led to a patch of woods.

"I hope that's where you were going, big guy," she muttered. She deposited the turtle in the grass. "Stay out of the road this time!"

Ellery and Janet were bouncing up and down in the car when Beth climbed back in. Cars passed on their left, drivers and passengers peering at them. But the girls' enthusiasm was unchecked. Beth had saved the day, and the afternoon of shopping was a happy interlude in an otherwise overcrowded life.

Beth was still hard at work for the most part, but she'd now moved on to the nursing program at Brookdale Community College. Despite her misgivings, she continued to occasionally go out with Gretchen and Michael, but she never felt easy about it. The whole bar scene turned her off, and she had to shut down her inner voice by scolding herself and telling herself to be normal.

That's what normal people do, Beth, she chastised herself. *They go out and they meet people. They socialize.*

Beth met people easily enough. Men were drawn to her beauty and kindness. The first guy she actually dated was a tall drink of water named Ralph. Ralph was an airline pilot who drove a Corvette. *What's not to like?* she thought.

She soon found out.

The silver Corvette glided into Beth's driveway, purring like a tiger. Beth was excited to go out with a man who moved in circles she'd never been part of. They had met for coffee on the first date; Ralph had taken her to dinner for the second.

The third date would be something Beth had never done before: She'd agreed to accompany Ralph to his weekly Alcoholics Anonymous meeting. Over dinner on the second date, Ralph had confessed that he'd had a drinking problem and taken a vow of sobriety. Beth thought even more highly of him for his vulnerability and courage.

A middle-aged man in a suit greeted Ralph and clapped him on the back. "Good to see you, buddy," the man said. Then he turned his attention to Beth. "Welcome," he said politely. "Is this your first time?"

Ralph turned around and spoke a little sharply, "It *is* her first time. She's my guest tonight."

"Great, glad to have you." He nodded a little too fast.

Beth raised her eyebrows, nodded once at the man, and followed Ralph to a seat. This was a speaker's meeting, so they sat in rows of chairs facing a dais.

Ralph clued her into the format of the speaker's meeting: "They're pretty inspirational. The speaker will be someone who's been sober for a while and who's willing to share their experience, strength, and hope."

A few moments later, a middle-aged man took the stage. "Hi. I'm Gary, and I'm an alcoholic."

Pretty soon, Gary had the audience engrossed in his tale. His delivery—fast and funny—brought to mind a stand-up comic, but the story's underlying poignance lent it gravity. Gary spoke eloquently about the entrenched beliefs he'd harbored in his drinking days and how, in retrospect, they were both wretched and amusing.

Drunk on a daily basis, Gary would start to feel a craving around 10 in the morning while at his desk in the office. Doing his best to fight off this creeping craving, he'd break into a sweat. Finally, he'd cajole himself to hang on till lunchtime when he'd have "just one" with his meal. Invariably, Gary would drink himself into a stupor then return to the office. There'd be more drinks at the end of the workday, and he'd be unable to make the long commute home from the city. Instead, he'd collapse in a cheap rented room for the night.

Over the years, Gary had learned about ways to "rehabilitate" his clothing night after night. He could make one suit last for days, he joked, if he rinsed out his underwear in the sink and hung it to dry, stood his socks up in the corner, and sprayed his button-down shirt with antiperspirant. The one thing that couldn't be seen two days in a row, he joked, was his tie. But it was New York City, and the local haberdashery opened at 7 a.m., probably for just this purpose. At the end of his drinking days, Gary had amassed quite a collection of ties, including several with outrageous patterns and colors.

After the meeting, Ralph and Beth got coffee at a local diner.

Recalling Gary's story, Ralph shook his head. "What a ne'er-do-well!"

Beth sat up straighter. "Ralph, how can you say such a thing? What happened to 'There but for the grace of God go I'?"

Ralph burst out laughing. "Oh, come *on*, Beth. Spare me the pious act. I was never *that* bad."

"You're an alcoholic, aren't you? Isn't that why you go to those meetings? Aren't you biting the hand that feeds you?"

Ralph fixed her with a disdainful look. "On the contrary, I pay my own way, and I control my own drinking." He motioned to the waiter. "Look, I'll show you."

A young man in a black dress shirt and trousers came over.

"I'll have a martini. Two olives."

Beth was aghast. "Ralph, no! You're undoing all the good you've done. Please, don't!"

"Relax, I do it all the time."

Ralph knocked back the martini and downed another, talking faster and louder by the moment.

Beth became increasingly concerned about where this night was going. "Ralph, I think I'd like to go home now."

"Nothing's stopping you." He ordered his third drink, barely looking at her.

On the taxi ride home, Beth reflected on the difference between Ralph's suave persona and his crass personality. *If I didn't know better*, she thought, *I'd think he has a mental illness*. Yet, curiously, it wasn't Ralph whom Beth mentally berated; it was herself—for choosing the wrong guy or at the very least for bringing out the worst in him.

She still had a lot to learn. Then again, she'd started way behind everyone else.

Chapter: Twenty-Three

Early the following Sunday, Beth, Ellery, and Janet emerged from St. Rose Church after mass into a fresh, sunny morning. Once again, the quiet of the sanctuary, the regular rhythms of mass, and the offering of peace from Beth's fellow parishioners had calmed her spirit. She could still feel the vibration of a hundred voices chanting the Our Father. The feeling of contentment, of the enigma beyond human understanding, lay warmly within her heart.

As she and the girls followed the throng of churchgoers from the narthex into the open air, Beth paused behind the men, women, and children descending the eight steps to the sidewalk. She watched as worshipers turned left and right, flowing along like a river. Colorful and purposeful, each person, with their own soul set right for the week, strode toward their destiny. Beth felt a kinship with every one of them. They were all doing their best—striving to be happy, to care for their loved ones, to make ends meet. She took a deep breath, descended the stairs, and joined them.

After a late breakfast, Beth drove to her cleaning job at a local condominium complex. Janet did some homework, then planned to go out for a bike ride. Ellery had a date with Artie that afternoon. They'd been seeing each other for over a year and a half, and things had grown serious between them. As Beth scrubbed out a tub that afternoon, her concerns about Ellery's relationship intensified. She had mixed feelings about Artie. She was happy because Ellery was happy, but she had a negative intuition about Artie. He seemed shifty.

As Beth went outside to empty the garbage, she was preoccupied and failed to notice the bee's nest inside the wooden lattice enclosing the garbage. The hive was unusually low, and she bumped into it as she stepped inside.

Beth heard a buzzing noise and felt a sharp sting. She didn't stick around to get a look at the insect; she just ran back inside.

What a day! thought Beth. *It started out peacefully in church. Then my worries were buzzing around in my head until I got stung by an actual bee. Thank God it's quitting time.*

As Beth was driving home, her arm began to throb where the bee had stung her.

Head hurts, too, Beth thought. The road was blurring in front of her, and the buzzing in her ears had grown deafening. *What's happening?* Beth saw a tunnel in front of her.

That can't be right. The tunnel was compelling. She felt drawn by an irresistible force, but she wasn't afraid. In fact, she felt comforted and safe. A crystal blue light appeared at the end of the tunnel. Beth was overcome by a desire to melt into the light, serene in the knowledge that it would give her the love and belonging she'd always sought but had never found.

In reality, Beth had missed her turnoff at Belmar Boulevard, crossed the yellow line, and crashed into a mailbox.

Janet had been outside a pharmacy. She'd seen her mother drive by and miss the turn. Although Beth's car was now out of sight, Janet heard shouts. She sprinted in the direction of the commotion and arrived on the scene to find her mother unconscious in the driver's seat and—it was almost surreal—her Uncle Ryan in the middle of the road, directing traffic.

An ambulance soon arrived. Despite Uncle Ryan telling everyone Beth had been drinking, the emergency room doctors discovered she'd had an anaphylactic reaction to the bee sting. Her heart and respiration had stopped, and she had come as close to death as possible without going through its gate.

Beth was out of work for a full week. Since she wasn't able to drive, Ellery and Donnie took her to the bank and did the grocery shopping. At the end of that month, Beth's budget had been skewed by a week without pay and the extra bills. Living in the big, beautiful home that gave each of the kids their own bedroom had been a stretch, but Beth had been determined to make up for the lean, early years, the lack of emotional safety, and their silent, neglectful father. She had been living paycheck to paycheck, and now the overdue notices began to feel like a tidal wave drowning her in debt.

Late one night, Beth sat at the dining room table with the bills spread out before her. She was tired and not thinking that clearly, but this was the only time she had to try and figure things out. With the kids sleeping, the rest of the house was quiet and dark.

Beth dropped the electric bill on top of her handwritten calculations and put her head in her hands. All she wanted to do was go to sleep. She'd been up since 5 o'clock in the morning, when she'd packed her lunch and dinner and written a note for the kids. Her shift at the hospital started at 6:45 a.m. and ended at 3:15 p.m. From there, she went to her cleaning job, which lasted until 9 p.m.

All right, she thought to herself, *slow down. "Don't just do something. Sit here."*

She'd learned that little nugget from a psychotherapist whose apartment she cleaned. She took a deep breath and faced the truth. She had to do something before things got past the point of no return. She would not give in to despair. She would not.

Chapter: Twenty-Four

As Beth watched from the front door, Donnie and his buddies closed the doors on a U-Haul truck and dusted off their hands. This was the last load of furniture and boxes from their Garfield Street home. Their new place in South Wall was a much smaller house whose financial demands Beth could handle more easily.

Ellery didn't join Beth and her siblings in the new house. She'd married Artie and the couple had moved into their own home. Beth and Janet each had their own small bedroom in the small house, and Donnie had half of the basement, which had been converted to living space. Since her mortgage had been cut in half, a crushing weight had been lifted from Beth's mind and heart.

Though it wasn't "cool," Beth owed much of her good mental health to her focus on spirituality. Although her friends were Catholic, they didn't observe the sacraments of weekly mass or prayer. Beth, on the other hand, had been praying the rosary ever since she'd made her First Holy Communion at St. Joe's. She still had her mother's wooden rosary beads, which Ada had given her 30 years earlier. Smooth and worn, those beads had comforted Beth as she'd sat in various places—sometimes placid, sometimes desperate, but always fervent in her supplications.

She sometimes looked back on her life with regret, especially when she reflected on her ruined marriage.

Donald never liked me going to church, she thought. *Maybe if I'd stopped going, we could have worked things out. But that's the only thing that really saved me. It was the only thing I had to lean on, the only constant in my life. A comfort. A source of strength.*

Beth was blind to some things, among them were her own strength and courage. She had grit. She was dedicated to her children, and she never forgot that lesson, that creed she'd first heard in St. Joseph's sanctuary so many years earlier: *Greater love hath no man than that he lay down his life for his friends.* It had pierced her heart like an arrow the moment she'd heard it and remained there ever since. It was a guiding light to her.

That light allowed love to return to Beth in the most natural way: while she was working on a medical-surgical floor at Jersey Shore. One of her patients turned out to be an old customer from Le Deauville Inn. George, a dentist, needed some minor surgery and—luck of the draw—was placed directly in Beth's path. During their brief conversations when Beth came to check his vital signs, Beth discovered that George was a widower with an adult son. Beth met his son, Gary, when Gary came to visit. She observed how the two interacted with love and humor. She liked what she saw. Before he was discharged, George asked Beth for her number and invited her out to dinner.

Beth was hesitant at first. She agreed to coffee. But after they spent hours talking about their pasts, their children, and their hopes for the future, Beth agreed to the dinner date.

George was a large man: six feet tall and built like a linebacker. He was average-looking until you had a conversation with him. He was a good storyteller, a great listener, and had a depth of wisdom that elevated his appearance.

Over the next two months, George and Beth tried several of the local restaurants. Beth discovered that George was a fish enthusiast, and they made a game of rating some of the most popular eateries.

After a few months of dating, George took Beth to dinner at Le Deauville Inn. What a different experience this was, to enter the expansive dining room with ruby-red Aubusson carpets and 30-foot ceilings as a guest! Beth felt the thrill of it. Sapphires dangled from her ears and a smile wreathed her face. George ordered a bottle of Pouilly-Fuisse to complement their sea bass dinner. Several of the employees came up to Beth to say hello and wish her well.

George enjoyed looking at Beth across the table. Her dark, wavy hair complemented her beautiful skin. Her cheeks were flushed, and her eyes sparkled. He imagined what life would be like if he could have dinner with her every night. *What am I waiting for?* he wondered.

He leaned across the table. "Beth," he said, reaching for her hand. "You look beautiful tonight." His gaze locked on hers, George stood, still holding her hand. "Beth," he gasped, feeling slightly short of breath. He knelt on one knee in front of her. She brought her other hand to her cheek, her beautiful mouth rounded in a perfect *O*. "Beth, will you marry me?"

Beth fell forward, wrapping her arms around his neck. "Yes, George! Oh, yes!"

Applause erupted from the tables around them. A waiter appeared with a magnum of champagne and two flutes. Beth felt she could not contain her happiness.

Beth and George both agreed that life was too short to wait. They married that June with all their children in attendance.

Beth and George were deliriously happy. George rented his home and moved in with Beth as she had wanted. They spent a week at the beach, lolling in the sun, reading paperback books, and talking over current events. Their happiness was short-lived, however. Before the end of that first summer, George was diagnosed with cancer.

Beth contacted her mentor, Dr. Grande, as soon as she and George got the diagnosis.

"Go to Sloan-Kettering," urged Dr. Grande. "They're the best game in town when it comes to treating cancer."

So it was that, in late August, the couple visited Memorial Sloan-Kettering Cancer Center in New York City, where they discovered that George had a virulent form of brain cancer called glioblastoma multiforme.

The surgeons at Sloan-Kettering urged immediate surgery due to the aggressive nature of the cancer, but the surgery itself was life-threatening. After the consultation, Beth and George clung to one another in the car in the parking lot.

George had surgery the following week and survived. The surgical team warned them, however, that glioblastomas often recur. George was scheduled for follow-up treatment three days later, which he could get locally.

After neurosurgery and a regimen of chemotherapy and radiation, George grew more and more gaunt. He lost his appetite and took little pleasure in anything. He died on Christmas Eve, but Beth felt she had lost him on the day of his surgery. How heavy was Beth's heart!

Maybe I'll just quit school, she thought as she trudged through her days that cold, empty winter. She felt that old worthlessness consume her. Her girls wouldn't hear of it when she managed to utter this aloud, so she held on for them. But her heart wasn't in it.

That winter, Donnie had taken a job at the local airport. He had his friends over for Saturday-night parties in the finished basement, but they were low-key. Janet, now 16, had started dating a young man named Patrick Kilcullen. The Kilcullen family lived in the neighborhood. The parents were divorced, and the kids lived with their father, who was a prominent businessman. Unfortunately, their mother was an alcoholic. Even though she didn't live with her ex-husband and the children, she dropped in and out whenever she wanted, often causing chaos.

Beth soldiered on through the bleak winter, held down all her jobs, and graduated from nursing school at the age of 46. A couple of weeks later, she traveled to Atlantic City to take her nursing board examination. She passed with flying colors. Here she was, the little girl whose parents had ignored and terrorized her, who had made her believe she was nobody's darling. Now she was walking down the aisle in the packed auditorium, resplendent in her white uniform and cap, to receive her diploma.

She'd already landed a job—it had been so easy her head was still spinning. On Monday she'd start her position on Two Lane, a medical-surgical floor at Point Pleasant Hospital in Point Pleasant, New Jersey. The hospital itself sat on a bend in the Manasquan River, and the views were magnificent. It was about time that life delivered something pleasant to Beth Miller Hoffman.

The excitement of the new job was overwhelming, but it also brought a welcome anticipation of the future and all that was possible.

Two Lane was a wild floor; you never knew what would happen next. One of Beth's first patients was a 300-pound woman who'd been slow to heal after surgery. When Beth asked her to roll onto her side so Beth could see whether she'd developed bedsores, the patient smiled. "I can't. You'll have to lift me."

Whaaat? Beth was strong but there was no way she could move this woman.

The first attempt, with three of her colleagues, was unsuccessful, particularly since the patient made no effort whatsoever to move so much as a muscle. Outside the door, the colleagues conferred and came up with a solution.

"Time for some traction," Beth announced as she rolled in a cart covered with splints, bandages, adhesive tape, and pulleys. Once she had the patient hooked up to the bars and cords, two other nurses helped Beth get the woman on her side. Problem solved.

Traction was unusual on Two Lane. A much more common occurrence was the admission of elderly patients who'd been sharing their medications. They did this mostly to avoid the high cost of their medicine, which forced some of them to choose between eating and having their prescriptions filled. (Beth had heard of senior citizens who relied on cat food or dumpster diving to fill their bellies.) Some, however, did it simply to be neighborly. Unfortunately, it did a lot more harm than good.

Virginia was one of those patients. She'd been sharing meds with her friend across the street in her over-55 community. And Virginia was well over 55. She was a frail, old gal and almost completely bald save for the feathery wisps crowning her pate. Because Virginia still had some of her youthful vanity, she wore a shaggy white wig over her feathery locks.

When she put her head down on the tray of her Geri-chair, her white mop flopped all over. Seeing Virginia in her usual position, Beth gently helped her sit up and gingerly swept the hair back over her head so she could see.

"Come on now, Virginia. Let's perk you up a bit. It's time for some hydration."

Virginia was still out of it from mixing inappropriate meds. She had an IV drip, but the staff was trying to get her to drink on her own. It made them sad to see the condition of some of their patients, so they did what they could to liven up their floor.

Making the best of their working hours, Beth and her colleagues often clowned around and played jokes on one another. Nora was the head nurse on Two Lane, so called because she had both supervisory and clinical responsibilities. She was often the instigator of the more raucous schemes, but the Two Lane team played their share of jokes on her as well.

"Hey! Nora! There's a new admission," Carol called from down the hall. "You'd better come—they might not be breathing!"

Nora rushed over to the hall bed. When she pulled back the sheet, she gasped and reflexively pulled back from the blown-up rubber glove with a magic marker face. The rest of the gang fell about the place laughing.

On another day, Nora prompted Beth and the others to tie up a nurse from a different floor—a "floater"—in a wheelchair and send her downstairs in the elevator. (Floaters are a symptom of a never-ending problem: the shortage of nurses. One way administrators handle it is to pull nurses from their assigned floors and place them on floors that are short-handed. The relocated nurses are called *floaters*.) Luckily, this floater—the daughter of a doctor—had a good sense of humor and didn't file a complaint with the administration.

Nora was a paradox. On one hand, she indulged in crazy stunts and pranks, but on the other hand, she was a good charge nurse and took care of her floor. For example, if the air-conditioning wasn't working, she'd call maintenance. But if no one came, she'd call administration and warn them, "The situation here is untenable for both the medical staff and the patients. If maintenance doesn't get here in ten minutes to fix this problem, I will issue a stop-work order for the entire floor." She'd always get her way in confrontations like these.

With all of this camaraderie and the frequent challenges, Beth was satisfied in her work. She'd made her dream of becoming a nurse come true. In her private life, she'd had two marriages that had ended badly, and was in no way looking for a new husband.

But her heart longed for a new source of comfort: grandchildren. She found ways to remind Ellery that she and Artie could give her grandchildren any time.

Donnie wasn't yet a candidate for fatherhood, since he wasn't seeing anyone. Janet had graduated from high school and had entered Rutgers University. It seemed that Ellery was her only hope for a grandchild in the near future.

Ellery wasn't ready, though. She was living a quiet nightmare. Artie had begun to act erratically. He had become paranoid, had purchased a pistol, and now kept it under his pillow. One night, Ellery awoke gasping for breath from a nightmare only to find Artie's hands around her throat. He had a faraway, manic gleam in his eyes as he screamed, "I'll throttle you, you bitch!" Ellery managed to call his name, and Artie snapped out of it. When he saw what he'd done, he began weeping and begging Ellery for forgiveness. She'd comforted him, but the trust she'd once had in him was gone.

Meanwhile, due to the nursing shortage, Beth was often pulled to other floors. She liked Two Lane but didn't relish being switched at that last minute.

One day Beth was assigned to the pediatric floor. Dealing with young children left her feeling uncertain and ill-prepared. She hadn't spent much time in "peeds" and had no special training for these little developing bodies. After all, when it came to medicine, children weren't just little people and often couldn't communicate what they needed.

On this day, however, Beth encountered a chatty toddler who needed a sponge bath. As she was washing him, he locked his dreamy angel eyes on Beth's and announced, "Oh, I like this!" Beth's heart turned over, and she knew this was her calling. Just like that. She pursued a transfer and pretty soon she was working there full-time.

Nonetheless, dealing with the injuries and illnesses of children was no lighthearted matter. One Easter Sunday, after Beth had worked her regular 7 a.m.-to-3 p.m. shift, she was eager to get home to her family. Donnie was still living at home, Ellery and Artie were coming for dinner, and, of course, Janet would be there. Family time was the best reward for Beth, and her heart was buoyant as she rounded the corner on her way out. Then she saw the slight figure lying on a stretcher in the hallway. A nurse and a doctor were urgently communicating as they moved over his body. The child looked about six years old.

Beth later learned that he, his brother, and his parents had been driving to their grandmother's house. Because their grandmother lived in the same neighborhood as they did, the parents had been lax about the boy's seat belt. Unbeknownst to the parents, the boy's car door had not been shut all the way. As they rounded a corner, it flew open, and he tumbled onto the asphalt. As Beth passed the stretcher in what felt like slow motion, her stomach clenched as if readying her for action. There was so much blood Beth could smell its metallic odor even before she reached him.

That's way too much blood, she thought. *He's going to die.* Just like that, she knew. She felt the emotional blow as if it were her own child. That was the cost of this career, the cost of caring. It was paid sometimes in sorrow, sometimes in anger at a parent's recklessness or negligence. A recurring theme that embodied parental carelessness was the innocent family dog.

How many times do we have to see this? Beth thought as she looked down at another little boy. The family dog, whose owners insisted he'd "never bitten anyone," had savagely torn his face, head, and throat.

Please, God, let this child live, she prayed.

He was white and still, but he was conscious, his trusting eyes watching as she and the doctor worked.

He might live, she thought, *but he'll never look the same.*

Dr. Kapili, the neurosurgeon, was so angry he was almost as pale as his patient. After examining the child, he'd taken the parents aside to discuss the child's condition. They listened to him dispassionately, occasionally murmuring that they hoped the dog was okay and that he was being treated properly by the authorities who had taken him away.

Dr. Kapili angered visibly. These two people hadn't protected their child from an animal they kept in their home. Because of their lax training and supervision, the beast had maimed the child beyond recognition. Yet the parents were more concerned for the dog than for the boy.

"Let me be clear," Dr. Kapili said. "This animal you're so concerned about is still in the best of health. Your son, however, has been hospitalized because your dog very nearly killed him. If that were my dog, I would destroy him before he had a chance to maim or kill some other defenseless person." With that, Dr. Kapili turned on his heel and strode down the corridor.

Like this little boy, each child who stayed in the pediatric unit had their own story to tell. Some were fairly routine cases, like dehydration from a bad stomach flu, or an appendectomy or tonsillectomy. Other cases, like this little boy, were compelling and stirred the emotions of the staff as much as they spurred the medical team to give it their best.

One of the hospital administrators, Ed Fischer, had taken notice of the competent and lovely brunette. A widower, Ed had looked up her file even though it wasn't necessary. He'd only heard good things about her, and her work didn't impact any of the issues he was overseeing in pediatrics. Nevertheless, he was curious. Asking around, he found out she was a widow.

Two peas in a pod, he thought. *Or maybe we could be*.

Ed was a traditional sort. He'd liked being married and had enjoyed providing a nice home for his wife. He had a grown stepdaughter but no children of his own.

Keeping an eye out for Beth, he managed to run into her in the cafeteria. He introduced himself and offered to buy her a cup of coffee.

"I'm sorry," Beth said, "but I have to get back to my floor. Maybe some other time …?"

Ed was determined to make sure there was another time, but he was careful not to seem pushy. He visited pediatrics once a week or so, and he would wave hello to Beth from a distance. She was worth waiting for.

A few weeks later, he invited Beth for a cup of coffee after work. She was in no hurry at the time. She had also learned more about him since his first invite. Ed had a reputation as a nice guy and a good administrator. He was financially and emotionally stable. She could let down her guard.

The two went out on a few dates and discovered they had a lot in common. He was intrigued by her life with the children and empathetic to her struggles as a single mother. She saw in him a man not used to living alone, doing his own laundry and cooking for himself. Nor was he happy living alone.

During her days, though, when she wasn't out with Ed, Beth was concerned about Ellery, who didn't seem very happy in her marriage. Nothing was said; it was more the tension she could feel when the young couple visited, which wasn't often, and the way Ellery would flinch when Artie touched her.

Not a good sign in any couple, Beth thought, *but even less so with a pair of newlyweds. Newlyweds were the reason the saying "Get a room!" had been invented. But not here*, Beth saw, *not here*.

Moreover, Ellery was putting on weight, another sign of stress or unhappiness. Add to that the sad expression on her daughter's face, and Beth felt the invisible weight of her daughter's distress around her own neck.

Despite her son's ready smile, Beth worried about Donnie, too. He was intelligent and sensitive but still masculine. Yet Beth wondered whether his father's absence and negligence had had a detrimental effect on Donnie.

He drinks a lot but is it too much, or is it just what young men do? I'm not really one to judge that well, not after what we lived through in our family.

The real surprise was that Janet was pregnant. Despite her youth—she was only 18—she and Patrick wanted to get married and start a family. *Imagine, the youngest is giving me my first grandchild!* Beth was cheered by the thought. After all, she'd been giving not-so-subtle hints about giving her some grandbabies. But Janet was so young, and she had dropped out of Rutgers University in her freshman year to get married. *And her husband ... would he straighten out and settle down?*

Patrick Kilcullen was a drinker. Not all that surprising since his mother was an alcoholic who'd left her seven children to drink in Sophia's Tavern in downtown Manasquan. It didn't bode well for the future. But there was only so much Beth could control.

Remembering a phrase from that long-ago AA meeting she'd attended, she told herself, *One day at a time, Beth. One day at a time.*

When she had time to herself, Beth often included Ed in home-cooked meals around the kitchen table in her Oak Road home. Ed, however, liked to have Beth visit him in his more spacious but empty-feeling home in Point Pleasant. One evening, after one of Beth's dinners, Ed popped the question. "Will you marry me? I would be very happy if you said yes."

Beth did not disappoint him, and the two tied the knot in a simple ceremony before going off on a cruise together.

Beth was determined not to interfere in her children's lives, to give them all the love and support she could, and to make the best of whatever came their way. What's more, there was a grandchild on the way—that was a light shining over everything.

Beth busied herself knitting a double-sided blanket to welcome the new baby, who was due mid-June. She chose yellow and white yarn colors since these colors would work whether the child was a boy or a girl. She was making good headway until she got a Sunday-morning call and was informed that the baby was already on its way—two weeks early.

Sunday's child is full of grace, Beth thought happily as she knit and purled in the lobby of her own hospital. Months earlier, after mulling over her choices, Beth had decided she wanted her grandchildren to call her Gramma. As she sat in the lobby on that sunny Sunday, some of her colleagues stopped to congratulate her.

"Hey, Gramma, you better finish up that baby blanket!"

Thanks to the morning call, the blanket was done by the time baby David was born on that bright June afternoon.

Beth was either caught up in her daily routines or the drama of moments like these. It made the years fly by. During that time, Beth developed a practiced automaticity in her career. She took everything in stride and could reassure her young patients and their parents while she was caring for them. Her professionalism had grown by leaps and bounds. She had gone from a somewhat shy and uncertain young nurse to an experienced and skilled expert. This almost always put her patients and their parents at ease. Beyond that, her kindness and generous spirit elicited gratitude. She always lent a hand, no matter how difficult the task. Nor was anything too menial if she saw a worker struggling. She knew the names of every housekeeper, every pediatrician, every specialist, and every physical therapist who walked these halls. She asked after their spouses, their children, their grandchildren. She knew their fears and their sorrows because she had a listening ear. Many a heart had been lifted by Beth's kindness. Because she was selfless, always thinking of others, Beth was well-loved throughout the hospital.

After Beth had spent seven years on pediatrics, she felt a shift inside. Something new was tugging at her. As with her change of heart about nursing children, this had happened not by design, but by accident.

People love to talk; they'll talk about the good, the bad, and the ugly. In this instance, it was good news that had spread. Beth had a reputation as a hard-working, compassionate nurse, so when the nursery was short-handed, the charge nurse asked to have Beth sent over for the day.

Beth was accustomed to caring for little people—her patients sometimes weighed only 25 pounds. The patients in this unit, though, were a far cry even from that. Only minutes old, they often weighed between five and nine pounds, but some were even tinier. And more fragile.

Beth never thought she could care more about patients than she did about the children on pediatrics. Whether a year old or 15 years old, Beth had a soft spot in her heart for them and a sincerity even the youngsters could see. They had been her patients for seven years now, and she'd been very happy.

When she was floated to a different floor, she took usually it with grace and enjoyed interacting with the patients, no matter who they were. It provided a nice change from her daily routine and made her all the more appreciative of the pediatric floor and its patients. But floating to the nursery was different. When she held that first tiny baby in her hands, a new thrill rushed through her like the shower of sparks from a sparkler. This tiny infant was dependent upon her. This mewling creature, whose whole self—physical, emotional, psychological—was being formed each moment, from now until adulthood. Beth felt the import of it. She marveled at these minutes- and hours-old human beings, at their survival instinct, how they demanded to be fed and held. While taking the babies' vital signs, weighing them, bathing them, and changing their diapers, Beth's heart flip-flopped several times. She felt as if this was where she belonged. She pondered it during her shift as she went about her duties.

Jolene, the charge nurse, immediately saw that the babies liked Beth. One of the regular nurses was envious of the way the colicky babies quieted when Beth rocked and shushed them. She was too rushed off her feet to be envious for long, however, since she, Beth, and the charge nurse were responsible for the entire nursery.

Toward the end of the shift, Jolene called Beth into her cubicle of an office. Beth was a little nervous since it wasn't typical to be asked to see the charge nurse at the end of your shift, whether on your regular floor or as a floater.

"Sit down, Beth." Jolene waved her toward one of the two chairs that barely fit into the seven-by-seven-foot office. "How did your day go today?"

"Fine, Jolene." Beth's brow furrowed. "Did I do something wrong?"

Jolene laughed, showing nice white teeth and laugh lines around her eyes. "No, not at all. It just seemed as if you really enjoyed your work today."

"Oh, I did."

"Tell me a little more about that. What did you enjoy? What did you notice?"

When Beth hesitated, Jolene added, "No detail's too small. I'm just interested."

Beth was thoughtful. "I'm used to working with children, but the babies …" She smiled and shook her head a little. "The babies are so tiny, so dependent, yet so miraculous! They're complete and compact human beings, yet they're still going to form in so many ways as they grow and change."

"Beth, I have a question for you." Jolene looked into her eyes. "We have an opening here in the nursery. Would you be interested in transferring?"

Beth's heart gave a great leap. That was all the consideration she needed. Two weeks later, she started in her new position in the Well-Baby Nursery.

Beth was happily ensconced in her new spot when her second grandchild, a granddaughter, was born in November of 1983. Louise Kilcullen arrived early on a Saturday morning, and Beth was able to pop right into the nursery and into Janet's hospital room for the first visit.

Gramma Beth wasn't the only one enthusiastic about Louise's birth. Ed, who had never raised a child of his own, was just as excited to welcome the little one. They could call him Pop-Pop or Pop for short. David and Louise had a standing invitation to his and Beth's Point Pleasant home. Since Ed had retired a couple of months prior to Louise's birth, Pop-Pop had plenty of time.

By the time Louise was six months old, though, Ed wasn't feeling so well. He went for some tests, and he and Beth were poleaxed when they learned Ed had colon cancer.

Is this all my fault? Beth wondered. *Do I give people cancer? Why am I being punished? I must be destined to be alone and unloved. I'm still nobody's darling.*

Of course, this evil avalanche of thoughts dated back to Uncle Ryan, who'd blamed Beth for Donald's cancer. Ridiculous words. Ridiculous and misplaced anger. Yet they'd found their mark.

Beth was determined to help Ed in any way she could, so she carried on as usual and put on a happy face for him. He, unfortunately, was suffering with the worst gastrointestinal symptoms and losing a lot of weight. Beth made sure he was comfortable. She washed the sheets, towels, and his clothes when he accidentally soiled them. She made him delicious meals that were easy to digest. And she went to the nursery each day to care for the babies.

One night, Ed woke her, gasping in pain.

"What's wrong? What is it?"

Ed was pale and his face was sweating. When Beth examined him, she saw that his abdomen was grossly distended.

"Ed, when was the last time you had a bowel movement?"

Ed hadn't been able to pass anything for a couple of days, but he hadn't wanted to trouble her. Now he was in severe pain and in danger of rupturing something.

Beth called the oncologist, who ordered her to get an ambulance and get Ed to the ER immediately. He'd have the surgeon meet them.

During the three hours that Ed was under the knife, Beth sat in the waiting room, rosary beads in her lap. Eyes closed, she clasped each worn wooden bead one at a time. Quietly, almost silently, she prayed. "I believe in God, the Father almighty, maker of heaven and earth … Our Father, who art in heaven, hallowed be thy name … Hail Mary, full of grace …"

She felt a hand on her shoulder. It was Dr. Bernstein. As she looked into his somber eyes, he explained that the tumor had been wrapped around Ed's bowel, strangling it. They had to re-sect the colon and give Ed a colostomy. There was a slender chance that in time this could be reversed. For now, he'd need follow-up radiation.

Beth bowed her head, and the tears flowed.

Chapter: Twenty-Five

"Smile!"

Ed held baby Louise close. She had enough curly blond hair to gather in a tiny ponytail at the top of her head, and she looked like a little cherub with her porcelain skin and rosebud mouth. His heart filled as he looked at her, so happy and full of life.

Meanwhile, Ed knew his own life was slipping away a day at a time. He'd had a five-week course of radiation therapy. They'd marked up his skin with red pens and focused the beams on exactly the right places. Afterward, his skin was red and burned and painful. Despite all their efforts and all Beth's care, he didn't improve.

He smiled for Beth, for the picture, for baby Louise and her brother, David. He was so looking forward to being their Pop-Pop, to crawling around on the floor with them and playing games. He hoped they'd look at this picture one day and remember how much he'd loved them.

"C'mon, Pop!" Little David was wearing his Superman pajamas. "Let's play Superman!"

Ed's great, white-toothed smile took over his gaunt face. "Here you go, Gramma." He handed the baby back to Beth. "I've gotta help Superman save the world!" By God, he wasn't dead yet.

Two weeks later, he *was* dead. He'd ended up back in the hospital and in a great deal of pain. As Beth stood vigil by his bed, family came one by one to say their goodbyes.

Afterward, Ed wept, wiping his eyes with his ever-present hankie. "Your kids," he said, "treat me like I'm their dad."

Beth couldn't speak around the lump in her throat. Sorrow with pride in her heart. Losing Ed was a desolate prospect, but she was proud and happy about the relationship he and her children had forged.

That night, Ed slipped away. Their family doctor commiserated with Beth in the hour of his passing.

"He was such a genteel man," said the now-elderly Dr. Sayers, wringing Beth's hand. The doctor's eyes had a desperate, sad brightness, as if he was full of ideas that might prevent Ed's death despite the fact that it was too late for that.

Beth functioned on autopilot, making funeral arrangements, wrapping up Ed's estate, and going to work. The only bright spot in her life was stopping by to see Janet and the kids. Since Janet and Patrick lived in an apartment building with a communal laundry room, Beth insisted on doing the baby's laundry. It served two purposes: making sure the baby's laundry was spotless and providing Beth with regular hugs and grandchildren time.

How do you heal, Beth wondered, *after being pummeled to the ground time after time? How do you go on when all your dreams of love have been stripped away? What can you fall back on when you never had your parents' love*?

Beth had plenty of grit, but now she felt exhausted and empty. She went through the motions day by day but had to summon the willpower to do so. It was not getting easier as she got older.

Food was a comfort. Chocolate or ice cream raised her mood briefly. But her home and her bed were empty, and there were no comforting arms to greet her at the end of her day.

Yet there was the peace that came upon Beth when she prayed. At night, when she couldn't sleep. When a wave of darkness washed over her during the day and not even the babies for whom she cared could provide her with fulfillment or a sense of purpose. And even when she felt completely empty and alone. This often drove Beth to her knees, where she wept, lonely and sad.

One cold, rainy, blustery Sunday, she woke up in the early-morning darkness, still lulled by that hazy, dream-filled world of sleep. Her bed was warm and cozy. The mattress and sheets felt soft, smelled fresh, as if they'd just been dried on the clothesline. She felt the beginnings of a smile—until reality took over. All of her emotional defenses came crashing down. Her body felt heavy and she didn't want to open her eyes.

Sunday, she thought. *It's Sunday. But I can't get up!* She burrowed deeper under the covers, tears starting to come. She let them, giving in to a tide of sorrow that swept thought away.

But only momentarily.

"Okay," she said to herself. "Today is Sunday. Mass is an obligation, so I need to get up. Don't I have a lot to be grateful for? A lovely home that's safe and warm. Four wonderful children and two grandchildren. A good career. My health."

She thought back, as she often did, to her younger self, all dressed up and sitting at mass in St. Joseph's. To that day, so long ago, when Father Flynn's message struck such a deep chord within her. The music had played in her soul time and time again. “Greater love hath no man than he lay down his life for his friends.” *And his family*, she added.

Beth pictured her grandchildren: David with his mischievous brown eyes and big grin, Louise with her doll-like appearance. She felt an ache in her heart—an ache that had been there for so long, the ache for love.

Beth would fulfill her obligations as she always did. Not out of duty today, but out of a sense of purpose. Her children and grandchildren needed her. She would go to Mass. She would move forward. Even if she could barely function. She wore a black dress, a black storm coat, and black pumps. No makeup. *I must look a fright*, she thought. But she didn’t care. *I look like a widow, but that’s what I am.*

Father Garcia took the pulpit to give the homily. His voice rang with a clarion note in the air as he read from the scripture. “Love is patient, love is kind. It does not envy, it does not boast, it is not proud, it is not rude, it is not self-seeking, it is not easily angered, it keeps no record of wrongs. Love does not delight in evil but rejoices with the truth. It always protects, always trusts, always hopes, always perseveres. Love never fails.”

As she listened to his voice and that ancient passage in the quiet company of other believers, Beth felt her spirit lifted up. She was healing, even if by degrees. *Yes,* she thought, *love is not self-seeking. I have much work to do yet in this world.* She smiled.

Chapter: Twenty-Six

"That's it, David," Beth said as the eight-year-old poured the pancake batter into a Mickey Mouse shape. "Maybe you'll be a chef."

Five-year-old Louise sat at the dining room table putting together a puzzle.

That little Louise is smart, she thought. *I'll have to get some new puzzles soon. That's the fifth one this morning and she's done already.*

After they'd enjoyed David's pancakes, Beth got out the face paint and a box of costume pieces. Pretty soon, the kids had dressed themselves as their favorite animals, and Beth had taken photos of them on the front lawn. Then she put on a Batman mask, and they played superheroes.

After an hour of fighting off the forces of evil, Gramma Beth said, "Okay, let's read for a while." Over the years, she had nurtured the kids' natural delight in reading by gifting them wonderful books for their home and keeping a different bookshelf just for them at her house. David and Louise each took a moment to choose a book, and Beth sat in her easy chair.

Whew! she thought. *I'm gonna sleep well tonight.*

Beth loved having the kids overnight. It helped her stay in the moment and fended off self-pity. Her biggest reward was how much the kids loved it. When they smiled up at her in sheer delight or with pride in some new skill learned or task completed, Beth felt her heart heal even more.

This is what love feels like, she marveled. *What a shame my parents missed out on this.*

It was an old wound, but Beth didn't dwell on it. She accepted that her parents had tried their best. She didn't judge them. But deep down inside, she still carried that core belief.

I'm not worth it.

I don't matter.

I don't deserve it.

She didn't articulate these thoughts to herself. Who would want to acknowledge them? But they interfered with her ability to love herself as she loved everyone else.

And there was no disputing that Beth loved everyone else. She tried to look at everyone and accept them as they were. That was harder at certain times than at others.

One of the hardships for Beth was that Janet's marriage had been rocky from the start. Her husband, Patrick, had descended into the depths of alcoholism. Worse, he was a mean and lazy drunk. In the beginning, Janet and Patrick had decided that Janet would stay home with the children and Patrick would work. But he never actually got up to go to work, preferring to drink himself into a stupor at night and ignoring the alarm clock in the morning.

There was always an excuse or someone to blame for his failings, usually Janet.

Finally, Janet took a job at a local newspaper. Despite the fact that she lacked a degree at the time, she was a gifted and creative writer. Janet signed up for the evening shift so Patrick would be home with the children.

One night Patrick didn't show up after work, so Beth had answered Janet's call to come sit with the kids. When Beth walked in the front door, she heard yelling from the powder room at the rear of the house.

"You whore! Look at you!"

"Janet! What's going on?" Beth called.

When Patrick and Janet emerged, Patrick looked sheepish. And drunk. Janet looked—

Oh my god! thought Beth but said nothing. The children were in the living room.

Janet's shirt was torn and her mascara was smeared, making her look like a raccoon. Her arm was bruised and swollen.

Beth looked at Janet.

"Why don't you go upstairs and change? I'll stay."

No other words needed to be exchanged.

After Janet had called to ask Beth to come sit with the kids, Patrick had finally arrived home, inebriated and angry at the world. He had torn Janet's shirt and rubbed her mascara roughly into her eyes. But Beth's presence was a stabilizing force; he wouldn't dare act up in front of her. He was too much of a child. It was better for everyone, the children especially, if Gramma was there and saw to everything.

But did anyone consider how Gramma felt? Did she feel like a stabilizing force? No, not really. She was wondering how alcoholism and violence had repeated themselves in the next generation. She wanted better for her daughter, for her grandchildren. She wished for a quiet night at home.

Janet was fighting to be calm and act normally. Patrick, his violence quelled by Beth's presence, was quiescent for now, and the children didn't seem to be affected.

Beth did the dishes. She made sure the kids got washed up and put to bed at a decent time. She read them each a story before sending them off to dreamland. Then, when she thought Patrick was sober enough to handle the children, she packed up and went home. She knew it was useless to reason with him.

Headlights flashed by as Beth drove the short distance to her condo.

What's Janet going to do if this keeps up? she wondered. *He could have really hurt her tonight. He only stopped because I walked in. What a coward! My God, he could've hurt the children.*

Beth hadn't given that possibility any thought because Patrick hadn't done that—yet. She flashed back to her own childhood, when Bill had grown big enough to defend their mother, and their father had taken out his drunken anger and frustration on Bill instead.

Whack! Whack! Dr. Miller's fists landed against Bill's body. Bill was only twelve years old but could no longer stand aside as his father assaulted his mother in their home. He was a stocky, well-built boy, but he was no match for his drunken, angry father.

Beth shook her head. There was no use dredging up the past and dwelling on these ugly memories. She prayed fervently for protection for her daughter and precious grandchildren.

A year earlier, Beth had moved into an over-55 community. As a widow, she didn't need her large home any longer, and her daughter and grandchildren had been living in a small apartment. She had mulled it over and decided to give her home to Janet so the grandchildren would have their own rooms and a yard to play in, in a quiet neighborhood. The choice had felt right to her despite the objections of others.

"Beth, do you know what you're doing?" asked a friend from church. "Why would you give up your beautiful home and move to a small place like that? Your kids have to make their own lives. They made their own beds. Now it's time to let them take responsibility for their choices."

Beth knew they meant well, but she couldn't enjoy what she had when people she loved were uncomfortable or needed something. It gave her joy to give. It was as simple as that.

Did it have anything to do with her deep-seated feelings of being undeserving, unworthy? Perhaps they'd played a part when she was married to Donald, and she gave up her dignity and suffered his misogyny and neglect. These days, however, her generosity was based more upon riding her life's purpose across the span of her years on earth and making the most of them.

She'd done something similar for all of her children. After Ellery's frightening marriage to Artie had ended in divorce, Ellery had moved back in with Beth, and in time had found another love. When Beth had moved into Ed's home after their marriage, Ellery and her new beau, Gordon, had asked to purchase the Oak Road house. Despite her misgivings, Beth sold it to them at a much-reduced price. She was later to regret that choice since Gordon turned out to be a violent drunk. The Oak Road refrigerator bore an indentation shaped like Ellery's head from one particularly nasty rage. When they separated, Ellery was unable to buy out Gordon's half of the house, so the drunken bastard ended up with a lovely home at a fantastic bargain. Not the outcome Beth had intended.

Donnie's marriage had been on a more even keel … for a while. Donnie took after Beth rather than his father. He was kind, giving, and tolerant. Relationships suffer, however, when one partner does all the giving and the other does all the taking.

Bonnie had three sons when Donnie moved into her home. The youngest was still in diapers. Donnie, a web developer who'd never married and had no children of his own, took to fatherhood like a fish to water. He became a father to Timmy, Jeff, and John.

As the years went by, Donnie continued to give and give; Bonnie and the boys continued to take. Although Bonnie had no job, she was a prolific spender and gave no thought to saving for the future. She'd even feed their three dogs high-quality cold cuts rather than buy them dog food. Meanwhile, she stayed at home, eating, smoking, and growing ever fatter.

Donnie dealt with all this with his usual good grace, finding things for which to be grateful and doing his best to enjoy his everyday family life.

One Saturday evening he and Bonnie came home to find that 17-year-old Jeff, the middle son, had broken into Donnie's gun safe, and stolen his guns along with the family's second car.

Staying true to course, Donnie tried to help. Despite being the victim of Jeff's crimes, Donnie paid for a lawyer to help Jeff stay out of trouble. But nothing was ever good enough for Bonnie. She smoked and ate and bitched. Finally, one day, she informed Donnie that she wanted a divorce.

"I found someone else," she said. "No hard feelings."

Donnie was aghast. He'd made this family his life's work. Not only wouldn't Bonnie discuss it, but she'd also wanted him out immediately. So Donnie rented a tiny room in the next town.

Bonnie wasted no time in hiring an aggressive attorney and garnishing Donnie's pay. She began to call him at work so often to complain about everything that Donnie lost his job. When he fell behind in his alimony payments, Bonnie got a warrant for his arrest. Terrified to leave the house, Donnie asked his mother for help.

Beth hired an attorney, paid his back alimony, and kept paying the divorce settlement and alimony payments until Donnie got back on his feet. This left little for herself, but she never complained. She simply continued to lay down her life for her children.

Did she ever wonder whether she should back off and let them handle their own messes? Did she ever resent how the needs of her grown children left her in a precarious financial position? She didn't seem to. Rather, she was grateful she was able to help make all of their lives more comfortable, more stable. She was happy in her one-bedroom condo, spending as much time with her family as she could. After all, her motivation had always been "you kids," as she would say.

Beth was just as kind to friends and strangers as she was to her family. She'd always pitch in to help in her community, and she was a good neighbor. But there was one neighbor who sorely tried her patience.

Jessica Jones had always been Beth's neighbor. Sort of. Her father, a local attorney, owned the condo next door, which was attached to Beth's. After her parents died, Jessica moved in. From the beginning, she established herself as a troublesome, complaining braggart who thought she was better than everyone else. Even gold-hearted Beth grew exasperated with her.

Beth was working in her garden one morning when Jessica came around the corner. No sooner had Beth greeted her than Jessica started in.

"Don't you think something low and colorful would be better than that butterfly bush you planted? You know my father would never have planted anything as scraggly as that. And it draws all those insects."

"They're called butterflies, Jessica."

Jessica waved her hand airily as she kept walking. "So common."

Jessica's arrogance was bad enough, but when she started hallucinating and acting crazily, things escalated to a whole new level.

Beth was watching the news one evening when images on the TV screen were replaced by an electronic snowstorm. She tried clicking the remote a few times. Nothing. She shut the TV off, then turned it back on. Nothing.

Beth sighed and got out of her recliner. Her knees and her hips were hurting after a long shift at the hospital. “Guess I better call the cable company.”

Hours later, the cable repairman explained that Jessica had cut the cable wires in her attic. The main cable ran through Jessica’s attic to the other three neighbors, whose condos were part of the same building. Jessica had refused to let him in at first, but after she verified his status by calling the cable company, he found the source of the problem. When questioned, Jessica said she had to put a stop to all that demonic programming. Her answer convinced the repairmen to reroute the main cable through Beth’s attic.

Jessica’s strange behavior continued, but Beth remained complacent about her arrogance and her oddities. There were worse things in life to deal with. Eventually, without a word to anyone, Jessica disappeared.

Beth was busy with her nursing career, her family, and her flower garden. She saw her children and grandchildren as often as possible, except for Barbara. Barbara remained angry in Los Angeles, regularly dumping on Beth in single-space rants that went on for pages and pages. Nevertheless, Beth was confident that, one day, Barbara would realize how much Beth loved her. She wrote to Barbara twice a week, sent her presents on her birthday and Christmas, and cash when she needed it. Beth prayed often for all of her family, including Barbara. She also took regular walks around her neighborhood. Besides being healthy, this activity brought her peace and joy. And, as always, she continued to be one of the pillars of the local church, albeit a quiet one.

She had lots of friends at Ascension Roman Catholic Church. She was a member of the MAGI, the Mature Adult Gathering in Christ, so named after the wise men who visited the infant Jesus. Beth was in her early sixties, and these were Beth's peers in the church community. The group hosted various activities during the year, including luncheons, lectures, and trips. Every Sunday morning, she picked up Christine, Mildred, and Stephanie and drove them to church. They had a lot of laughs together.

Yet there was always that hole in Beth's heart. Alone in her home, she felt bereft. When she left a family event at Janet's house, she would cry from loneliness. Even if she rarely recalled her parents' fights or their neglect, she felt that ever-present, cold center, as cold as the Miller kitchen had been when she was a little girl. Deep down inside, she still felt like nobody's darling.

Beth's quiet time in prayer still soothed her when she felt this way. The sacraments of Communion and Mass gave her life and her spirit a continuity, a predictability that had been missing in her childhood.

As she was exiting the church one day, she looked up to find a dark-haired man at her elbow. He wore glasses and a tweed jacket. He smiled. She had often seen him in church, sitting alone. But they had never spoken before.

"I hope you don't mind if I walk out with you. My name's Herb."

Thus, it began, so simply. Beth enjoyed Herb's company. He was a widower, financially sound, and a family man with grown children and grandchildren. He was looking for a companion, and Beth was lonely.

Herb showered Beth with presents, many of which she didn't want. There was the burgundy Cadillac, for instance. He wanted her to have a fancy car to drive around in. She hated feeling like a showoff and wasn't happy about the car's thirsty gas tank and pricey repair bills.

Then there was the computer. It was the early 1990s, and he wanted her to be up to date with new technology. She thanked him but wasn't interested in communicating with anyone via email or surfing the internet. She liked to write long letters with a pen and paper.

These differences didn't matter, though. What did matter, over time, was Herb's constant carping about everything. If they went out to dinner, the steak wasn't cooked right. The seasoning in the potatoes was overbearing. If they took a trip together, it took forever to get there, and anyone they met on their journey was immature, rude, or looked at them funny.

It was finally too much for even Beth to tolerate, and she gave Herb his marching papers.

Chapter: Twenty-Seven

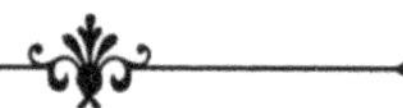

Beth walked along in her neighborhood in the fresh spring air. The sun was shining, and her heart was full. Beautiful flowers had burst forth under the clear sky. Daffodils and forsythia festooned fences and garden beds. Robins scampered across green lawns, watchful for worms to bring back to their nests. Beth's world had righted itself. She had purpose in her days now, and her nights of grieving were mostly behind her.

I have a lot to be grateful for, she thought. Mentally, she ticked off those things: her career as a nurse, which she had once only hoped for but had been able to make a reality; her children were alive and well; and she had two grandchildren who were healthy and happy. Being a grandmother was a delight. It offered the fun and marvel of watching children grow without the constant stress and worry of trying to feed and clothe them on a younger woman's salary. It had also alleviated a gnawing ache in her heart.

Beth pictured the smiling faces of her grandchildren now as she walked. They were so sweet and funny, and they shared their love without reservation. When she came to pick them up, or when Janet brought them over, they'd run to her, shouting, "Gramma!"

No wonder they loved Gramma's house! They made tents to play and sleep in, and Gramma would get in there with them. They watched movies and ate popcorn and stayed up late on Friday and Saturday nights. Gramma would pretend to be Batman while David was Superman and Louise was Batgirl. They had masks and a box of wigs, capes, and other costume items to outfit themselves as superheroes, villains, or other sorts of dramatic figures.

Beth sometimes wondered where she'd learned how to be a grandmother. It certainly wasn't from Ada, she thought, as she felt the old wound throb. No, Ada had had nothing to do with her own children, let alone her grandchildren. Ada had moved as far away from Beth and her children as it was possible to live in the United States—all the way to California. Inexplicably, she had moved in with a Mexican family, a single mother with three daughters. Ada acted as their *abuela—their* grandmother—and helped Juanita, the mother, raise the girls.

Beth's heart twisted. *I could've used that help*, she thought. Why hadn't Ada come to live with her to help her raise *her* children? After all, they were Ada's own flesh-and-blood grandchildren.

Beth put those thoughts out of her mind; that door was closed. She had to let go of the past even if it still had the power to wound her. She would be her own woman; she would be the kind of grandmother she herself would have liked to have.

A fresh gust of wind lifted her hair gently. Beth continued her walk and her "gratitude attitude." It was a trendy catchphrase, but focusing her mental energy on what she appreciated really did help lift her spirits. Beth added her church family to her mental list of things to be grateful for. She'd been attending Ascension Church for years now, ever since she'd moved into her Shore Drive condo, and she was more involved with the church now than ever before.

She and her friend, Eleanor, made coffee every Sunday for the early Mass. Eleanor was an early riser like Beth, and the two kibitzed and laughed while they set up the coffeemaker, cups, napkins, spoons, creamers, and sugar. During the week, Beth and the friends she drove to church walked and had get-togethers at each of their homes on a rotating basis. At Thanksgiving and Christmas, Beth helped raise money and supplies for the food pantry and helped pack up the holiday food baskets for the needy. She helped set up the Christmas tree in the church lobby and deck it out with "boy" and "girl" tags so that willing parishioners could contribute toys for children from families who were in dire straits. Beth loved Father Bernard, the Filipino priest who'd come to the parish. He'd helped move the parish of Ascension into a new era. Father Bernard's size—he was a diminutive 5' 4"—belied his expansive personality. He never met a human he didn't like. He made friends everywhere he went, and he was a great storyteller with natural enthusiasm but also a great listener when it came to needy parishioners. He was a gem.

There was only one thing missing from Beth's life: a partner and companion. But by 62 years old, Beth had developed a phobia about romantic relationships. Deep down inside, she believed she was bad luck, that a happy marriage wasn't in the cards for her. After all, hadn't she tried three times? The third go-round hadn't been the charm for Beth; it had been a death knell.

Men had shown interest in her, some of whom were even within the church family although she couldn't always be sure whether or not their intentions were romantic. A younger man who liked to sit with her during Mass fell into this category. They told each other stories like old friends and shared the details of their weekly lives. Larry was a tall, slender man with dark hair whose eyes lit up when Beth arrived to sit with him in the pew. A wine salesman, he always dressed well for Mass, usually in tan slacks and a navy sport coat. Larry traveled around the tri-state area and had many clients. Sometimes he took business trips to California to the wineries he represented and had even traveled to Italy when three of his wines were entered in a contest. They hadn't won any prizes, but they did get an honorable mention, he told Beth, and that was prize enough.

Larry was very interested in Beth's work in the nursery. He'd never married, so he had no experience with babies. He thought her work was marvelous. "I don't know how you do it," he said one Sunday. "I'd be terrified to touch them."

"Oh, no you wouldn't," she said. "You just haven't had the chance. I'm sure you'd take to it quite easily."

Beth wanted to reassure Larry, who was in his early forties. Who knew? Perhaps he'd meet a woman, fall in love, and start a family. He wasn't over the hill yet. Besides, a man's fertility had a much longer shelf life than a woman's. He just had to fall in love with someone who was still young enough to bear children.

People noticed the pair were always engaged in lively conversation and never ran out of things to say to one another. "Maybe," someone remarked, "Larry has more of an interest in you than you think."

Beth laughed until her belly hurt. "He's young enough to be my son," she exclaimed.

Eyebrows went up, but Beth paid no attention.

The years went by and kept paying dividends to Beth. She had invested so much in her career and her family; it only made sense that she'd see a return.

Janet had divorced Patrick after years of emotional and physical abuse and had gone back to school. Always a brainiac, she graduated with highest honors from college, went on to study at New York University, and became a lawyer. During those years, Beth had been on hand to help out with the children when needed, cooking for them, supervising their homework, and putting them to bed.

Ellery had found Jason, a man with whom she worked. The two had a lot in common, and she was much happier now than she'd ever been. They moved in together and spent a great deal of time landscaping their property and improving their home. They loved to drive around to different antique shops and what they called "the chicken coops," where they'd find great old furniture that they could restore for their home. Over time, they amassed a collection of grandfather clocks, 18 in all, that added to the coziness of their home.

Once Donnie had healed up over his divorce from Bonnie, he started dating the modern way—online—and found a perfect match. The only problem was that

Patty lived in Virginia. Luckily, Donnie liked to drive and spent most of his weekends on the long and winding road to visit her. It didn't take him more than a few months to pop the question, and soon Beth had a new daughter-in-law.

Things settled a bit more after Janet became a lawyer. She'd taken a position at a large law firm and developed a reputation as an effective litigator. Then she met Henry, superintendent of a large public school district. The couple married two years later and, combining Janet's two and Henry's three children, formed their own Brady Bunch.

Tragedy struck the newly merged families when the oldest daughter, the beautiful Julia, died suddenly from cardiac arrest. She was only 31. The medical examiner ruled that the fatal episode was brought on by an asthma attack. Despite emergency medical technicians pulling out all the stops, they were unable to save her life.

This catastrophe swept through the family, wounding each member in a different way. Julia's sister and brother were bereft. They had looked up to their older sister as a kind of second mother, especially since their own mother was mentally unstable and had been neglectful. David and Louise were shocked and saddened that their new siblings had suffered such a loss.

Henry and Janet pulled together to support each other and their children. One way they did this was by seizing the moment. After Julia's funeral, Janet and Henry gave each of the children a piece of paper and a pen. "Write down the top three places in the world you would like to go," they said.

Each list included Ireland.

Henry and Janet had learned the hard way not to delay dreams. They wanted their kids to see Europe and understand how good their life was in the United States. They planned a trip to Ireland and invited Beth to come along.

A few months later, the whole family piled into a big green Mercedes van at Shannon airport. It was the largest vehicle you could rent without possessing a commercial license, and the family was just able to squeeze into it—all nine of them. The gang included a fiancée and Henry's 90-year-old mother, May.

Driving in Ireland, despite being on the opposite side of the road, was a rush for Janet and Henry. What became challenging and even downright terrifying were the narrow roads, the habit of oncoming Irish drivers to pass vehicles and head straight for them, then veer back into their own lane at the last moment while waving a feverish *thanks* accompanied by a sincere smile.

The worst, though, were the signs with big black circles. They were posted anywhere there'd been a fatal motor-vehicle crash. There were a lot of them, and the signs enumerated exactly how many people had died in the spot Janet and Henry happened to be driving past. It was nerve-racking.

But beyond that, it was one wise-cracking, free-for-all of fun. They stayed with Mary Kearney from Killarney on her sheep, dairy, and tillage farm. The back door looked out on none other than the Gap of Dunloe. Mary welcomed the family to her comfortable farmhouse with freshly made scones and Irish tea.

They toured all over: the Dingle Peninsula, Muckross House, Lough Leane, Ross Castle, Dublin, and Galway. One night in Dublin, they all went out on the town for dinner. Then the young folks went to find the nightlife in Temple Bar; May stayed at the bed-and-breakfast to rest; Henry, Janet, and Beth went to Ned O'Shea's Pub.

The band was setting up in the pub, and the Irish clientele was charming to their American visitors.

One man, who was paying particular attention to Beth, leaned over to talk in Janet's ear above the noise in the lively pub: "My name's Aidan." Aidan had white hair and twinkling blue, blue eyes. "That's yer mother?" he asked in his delightful accent.

When Janet replied in the affirmative, he smiled and said, "Aye, yer mother's a beautiful woman."

While the bodhran, flutes, and fiddles played, Aidan flirted outrageously with Beth but remained a gentleman throughout the evening. Beth emerged from this experience with a big grin and sparkling eyes. It was a festive way to cap off the trip.

Before the end of the trip, though, there was another special moment for Beth. As they waited at Shannon Airport for their flight home, Janet pushed a small package into Beth's hands. She carefully unwrapped it to reveal rosary beads of Connemara marble. Overwhelmed, Beth clutched them to her chest. These marble beads, of varying shades of green, would always remind Beth of the Emerald Isle's windswept beauty and love of family.

When Beth returned from the trip, she cherished all the memories she'd made, including her memories of the lively pub music and Aidan with the twinkling eyes. Beyond that, however, Beth no longer had any interest in romantic relationships. She stayed busy with family, friends, work, and her church activities.

Church is more than just a once-a-week event, she thought. *Church is the people, the mystery of the Mass, the body of Christ through the outreach of his people*. Church was the holy way she felt during prayer time while she said her rosary. Church was a synonym for communication with her Creator, who'd saved her each and every time she'd needed something or someone. Church was a deep, devout communication with her inspiration, the spirit within her and the spirit within every other human being on the planet.

While the church played a constant role in her life, the role her profession played was changing. After decades of providing quality medical care to her patients, Beth left her nursing career and transitioned into a job working as a paraprofessional aide with preschool children who had disabilities. Beth had all the qualities that they needed and then some: she was patient, kind, funny, had a quick mind, and was a medical professional. Not surprisingly, teachers in the Swinton Falls school district fought over her.

Beth spent a few years in the classroom before she finally called it quits. Never one to sit around, though, she took a job at her local Walmart, where she ended up in the fabrics department. She rapidly made good friends among her colleagues, such as Lillian, an older woman with flowing white hair who stood about four feet high but made up for what she lacked in size with a big personality. Sandra was 70 years old, the same as Beth, a good solid woman of average build, brown hair going gray, and tortoiseshell glasses.

Both Lillian and Sandra enjoyed working with Beth, who did more than her share. She always had a smile and a kind word, and she was quick with a joke or a laugh.

Walmart turned out to be as interesting a workplace as the hospital. The clientele was varied and colorful, and there was never a shortage of escapades. One middle-aged man decided to shop in his boxer shorts. When the manager asked him to return after putting on a shirt and pants, the customer left the store and, stark naked, took a shower with Walmart's plant hose in the parking lot.

When a young woman was turned away from the ladies' room because it was being cleaned, she sneaked into the back of the fabrics department and did her business right in the aisle. *Clean up in fabrics*! The woman hid her face from the camera as she relieved herself so she couldn't be caught and charged. But she didn't realize that the camera outside the ladies' room had captured her image minutes before her misbehavior. Busted!

One of Beth's regular customers returned a roll of gingham fabric ribbon. The reason? It was haunted, she said. After she brought it home, it began emitting a dangerous aura. She warned the customer-service clerk to dispose of it properly or they'd all be harmed. The clerk brought it back to Beth, who, instead of exorcising the gingham ribbon, quietly said a prayer for the customer.

What a way to pass the time!

Beth continued to drive her friends to church every Sunday. It was a ritual to which they all looked forward, but as time flowed on, it brought chilly news on its currents.

Early one morning, Stephanie's next-door neighbor heard Stephanie's dog barking frantically. The neighbor knocked on the door. When she got no answer, she let herself in with the key Stephanie kept under the mat. She found Stephanie lying on the floor. She'd suffered a stroke, and although she eventually came home from the hospital, she would never be the same. She wasn't even able to return to church.

And so, the caped Sunday crusaders were down to three: Beth, Christine, and Mildred.

A few years later, Christine was diagnosed with pancreatic cancer. In no time at all, Beth and Mildred donned their best black dresses and went together to pay their last respects to their dear friend.

Two years after that, Mildred suffered a series of falls, and her family moved her into an assisted-living facility. Beth visited her once a month, and they had a grand time telling tall tales, reminiscing about the good times, and sharing family news. When Mildred was diagnosed with lung cancer, the doctors discovered her heart wasn't strong enough to withstand the proposed surgery.

"I'm glad," she told Beth one day on the sly. "It makes it easier for me. I didn't want the surgery, but my daughter would've tried to force me into it." Mildred waved her hand as if dismissing the idea. "This way the decision is made for me."

It was a sad day for Beth when Mildred passed on and she went alone to the funeral parlor. She was the only one left, the sole survivor of the caped Sunday crusaders. As she knelt on the velvet bench next to the coffin and looked into Mildred's face, a tear trickled down her cheek. "I'll miss you, my friend," she said softly.

Bad things are rumored to come in threes, so Beth figured that the bad news would take a rest now that her three closest friends had died. Unfortunately, it didn't quite work out that way.

When Donnie and Patty decided to relocate to Orlando, Florida, Beth suffered a psychological blow. Patty's adult daughter had settled there after attending college, and Patty wanted to be closer to her only child. It was more than reasonable, and Beth didn't begrudge them the move, but that didn't ease the heartache. She truly believed she would never see them again, and she spent many nights lying sleepless in her bed. Her reaction might seem extreme, but Beth's childhood experiences with poverty and alcoholic parents had made her sensitive to emotional losses and less able to feel as though she could do something about them (such as buy a plane ticket). Not to mention, at 85, her increasing lack of mobility.

As the years passed, Beth had more and more trouble with the arthritis in her hip and back. Louise, now fully grown and a degreed professional, urged Beth to use a cane. Beth would have none of it. If she was able to manage under her own power, by golly she would.

As Beth was leaving early Mass one frigid Sunday in January, she slipped and fell on the icy sidewalk. Rolling over, she checked herself carefully and, believing nothing was broken, got to her feet and made it to her car. No one had seen her fall.

It was her first fall but not her last. No sooner had she conceded to the cane than lymphedema set in, and she had to receive wound care at the hospital. This was frightening for Beth and her family since the Covid-19 pandemic had set in and going anywhere meant taking your life in your hands, especially for the elderly with health-compromising conditions.

The lymphedema caused Beth's legs to "weep," a condition caused by an inability of the body to move enough lymph fluid out of her lower extremities. As a result, her legs swelled and in some places the fluid created blisters. The blisters would burst, and the lymph fluid would ooze down her legs. Not only was this painful, smelly, and unsightly, but it created a heightened danger of infection. Nonetheless, Beth soldiered on as she always did. She wore her mask, sanitized her hands, and got on with it.

By this time, a number of other things had changed in the family. Ellery's Jason had lost his battle with cancer. Grandson David had married and taken a job with the New York Police Department. Janet's husband, Henry, had retired, and Janet had negotiated a remote, part-time job with her law firm. Janet and Henry had sold their family home, which had been within walking distance from Beth's condo, just around the corner and across from Ascension Church. Granddaughter Louise had purchased her own condo less than two miles from Beth.

In October of that year, just after a visit to the doctor, things took another bad turn. Despite Beth's difficulty with mobility, she'd driven herself to her appointment in her spiffy Toyota Camry. After her checkup, Beth sat in her car eating a banana and watching a North Jersey Coastline train rattling past on the tracks. *I feel like a normal person today*, she thought. It was a good feeling amidst the toils and obstacles she'd faced lately.

The following week, Beth started feeling under the weather—a little nauseous, unable to keep food down.

It's probably just a virus, she thought. Still, she mentioned her symptoms to Janet and Henry when they called on Thursday.

"When did this start?" asked Janet.

"Oh, let's see. Since about Monday, I guess."

"If it lasts much longer, Mom, you should go to the hospital and get checked out."

Beth demurred as usual. She was used to plowing through obstacles and persevering until she'd succeeded.

Henry, a wise counselor, added his thoughts. "Mom, you know I've gone to the hospital when I needed to. You baked me that coffeecake after I had my appendix out. But you're a nurse. You know the older we get, the more difficult it can be to shake something. What advice would you give to someone who's 89 years old and having your symptoms?"

"I know, I know."

Janet could hear Beth smiling—Beth knew she was being stubborn, and she knew Henry was right.

Chapter: Twenty-Eight

Janet's phone rang at 11 p.m. the next night, Friday night.

"Janet, it's Ellery. I'm at the hospital with Mom."

Beth still had not been able to keep any food down and called the ambulance. When the paramedics arrived, she asked them to take her to urgent care. But when the EMTs found out her age, her symptoms, and how long her symptoms had lasted, the driver said, "Ma'am, we're taking you to the ER!"

When the results of the CT scan came in, along with Beth's elevated white blood count, the surgical team whisked her into an operating suite. After several hours of surgery, Dr. Sharp approached Ellery in the waiting room. Ellery stood up, twisting her hands.

Dr. Sharp stopped in front of her in his green scrubs and surgical cap. "Your mother had an old hernia, which strangled part of her small intestine. It was completely dead. I had to remove it and re-section the rest."

Ellery held her breath.

"It's touch and go at this point, but if she survives the night, she should be fine."

Chapter: Twenty-Nine

Dark images swirled in Beth's mind, stirring an unnamed dread. The pain in her belly was so sharp, so deep.

When will it stop?

She twisted and writhed but couldn't get comfortable.

Why can't I move?

Background noises became clearer.

What's that smell? I know that smell...

Beth's eyes opened, but her vision was blurry. She felt confused.

Where am I?

Gradually, her vision cleared. Ellery was sitting on a chair nearby. But it wasn't *Beth's* chair. She looked around the room, and everything clicked: the noises, the smells, the pain, the surroundings. *Oh my God, I'm in the hospital!*

Ellery looked up and met Beth's gaze. Her eyes filled with tears, and she was at the bedside in an instant. "Mommy!"

Beth felt herself engulfed in an Ellery-scented hug. After spending the night at the hospital and hearing that it was "touch and go," Ellery's anxiety released itself in a flood and the whole story rushed out.

Beth was shocked to hear that she'd had an intestinal resection, but she was still bleary and disoriented, and the pain was dulling her senses and her ability to concentrate. In short, she was out of it. She was connected to an NG tube, so anything that was in her gastrointestinal system was going into a transparent container. Mostly green bile, and plenty of it.

The next day, despite her discomfort, Beth sat up and wrote out all the Halloween cards for her grandchildren and great-grandchildren. All the while, the NG tube ran up her nose and down her throat. It hurt to talk, and she couldn't sit all the way up. She leaned against her pillows, propped up like the Leaning Tower of Pisa, and wrote in her neat script on all those orange pumpkin cards, one for everyone, including the two newly arrived babies—her great-grandchildren.

The surgery wasn't the only thing threatening Beth's life. The Covid-19 pandemic was at its height, and there was no known effective treatment for the disease, only masks for prevention. The highly transmissible virus had already killed more than 100,000 Americans, more than had been predicted. The hallways of the hospital were festooned with banners and posters paying homage to the brave doctors and nurses—indeed, all of the hospital staff and first responders—who were risking their lives just by showing up to their workplace every day.

Eight days into her hospital stay, Beth was still in pain and not doing well. The staff had tried to remove her NG tube, but anything Beth ingested—which wasn't much, only broth and pudding—was coming right back up. The NG tube went back in.

More bad dreams, thought Beth. An apparition appeared at the end of her bed, a creature in a long, black cape with no face, only eyes—huge eyes and wild hair, like Medusa. Those who gazed into her eyes would turn into stone, Beth remembered.

Dear God, don't let me look into her eyes! she prayed. *I'm ready to die. I've lived a good life. Isn't it time to take me?*

The creature was speaking.

Huh?

"Hi, Mom." It placed a bouquet on her bedside table and removed its demonic cloak, which turned out to be a long, black raincoat.

Beth felt relief course through her body and closed her eyes for one fortifying moment. *It's Janet! I'm not crazy and I'm not dying.*

"It's raining cats and dogs," Janet said, "What a Halloween!"

What a Halloween is right, thought Beth. *With my own haunted hospital room!*

A week later, Beth was deemed fit to leave hospital care, but she wasn't ready to return home. Off she went to spend 19 days in a rehabilitation center. The ride was not pleasant. The transport didn't arrive until 7:30 in the evening, and the air was frigid. The burly driver tried his best to ease her off the hospital bed into the wheelchair, but he ignored her suggestions and ended up hurting her. He wrapped her up in the flimsy hospital blankets, covering her head with one of them.

Upon Beth's discharge after those 19 days, the director of the rehab was adamant: Beth could not return home alone, and there were virtually no services available.

Welcome to medical care in the good ol' U S of A, Beth thought, *only the richest country on Earth.*

Janet dove in and contacted all the potential providers. In the meantime, while they were figuring out the long-term plan, Janet and Ellery agreed to tag team each other, four days on and four days off.

Before too long, however, Ellery couldn't keep it up. She'd lost her husband just two years prior after having cared for him during his two-year battle with cancer. She'd taken him to all his surgeries and doctor appointments. Toward the end she'd changed his diapers, and she was with him on his deathbed. It was simply too much of an emotional toll to go through something like that again.

In the meantime, Beth's body let her know it was not happy with the surgeon's having removed part of it. It was acting up, sometimes painfully. Sometimes it simply refused to work.

Janet contacted the surgeon's office. The physician's assistant advised Beth to take mineral oil to keep the internal tracks lubricated and running properly. She said, "Give it a couple of days. It should straighten out. But if it doesn't, call back any time."

The day before Thanksgiving, Beth was still stopped up, so the PA adjusted the dosage of mineral oil and Colace, an over-the-counter laxative. "That should do the trick," she said.

Thanksgiving arrived. Since it was the middle of

the pandemic, Beth had a small gathering at the house. Janet and Henry had stayed over and put the turkey in the oven early.

By mid-morning, Janet realized that Beth was constipated. Under Janet's cross-examination, Beth admitted she hadn't passed anything for days.

Another call to the doctor. The doctor on call said, "She needs to go to the emergency room. She's probably impacted. If she doesn't get medical attention, her bowel could rupture. Not only would that likely be fatal, but it would also be very, very painful."

But Beth didn't want to go. She'd just spent 19 days in rehab and, before that, 14 days in the hospital. It was too much! She just wanted to be in her own home with her family on Thanksgiving.

But Janet was immovable.

The ambulance came once again and loaded her into the back. Janet watched with a wrenched heart, wondering whether it would be the last time she'd see her mom. She and Henry watched the ambulance depart and reluctantly turned back to the condo.

What to do now? They could not go to the hospital and wait outside the ER; no one was allowed into the hospital during the pandemic unless they were a patient. They decided to continue with Thanksgiving-dinner preparations.

Three hours later, the hospital called and said Beth was all set to be picked up. Hallelujah! A Thanksgiving miracle! Janet and Henry zoomed over to the hospital. Janet donned a mask and was directed to Beth's bed.

What an experience! No one ever wants to go to the hospital. It's not fun, and people die there. This time, beyond the usual prohibitions, Covid was stealing lives like nobody's business. And the virus was mutating before the scientific community could figure out how to eliminate it. Fear was everywhere. The ER doctors and nurses were gowned, gloved, and masked. It was a fearsome sight to behold.

Then there was poor Beth, all alone in her curtained cubicle. "That was the worst experience of my life," she told Janet. Yet she was smiling and grateful to the short, pleasant Dr. Cho, who had dug her hardened stool out of her bowels.

"Worst one ever!" he said. "Mom is a trooper." He patted her hand.

And off they went. Beth got into the Highlander, they backtracked to the condo, and Ellery arrived in time to meet the turkey as it came out of the oven. The day was balmy, so they were able to open the windows, sit six feet apart, and give thanks that it was all behind them.

Or so they thought.

One night on Janet's watch, she was awakened by a *thump*! and Beth calling her name. Leaping out of bed, she found Beth on the bathroom floor, unable to get up. Beth had gotten up with her walker and gone to relieve herself when her knee gave out and she fell.

Quickly assessing the situation, Janet knew she would be unable to lift Beth off the floor. She had Beth scooch out to the living room near the couch. After trying to figure out just how to get Beth on her feet, she realized that YouTube had videos for anything. Sure enough, there was an instructional video on how to help an elderly person get up after a fall. Go, YouTube!

Unfortunately, step one required the fallen person to get onto all fours. Due to her arthritis stiffness and pain, Beth was unable to manage this. Beth's hip was especially painful; her hip socket had been bone-on-bone for years. She should have had a hip replacement years earlier.

Did any doctor ever tell her that? Janet wondered. *Did she just dismiss it outright? Did she ignore her own needs to attend to everyone else's? Could she out of habit have failed to hear a doctor's recommendation?*

No one knew the answers to these questions, but they no longer mattered. At Beth's age and in her condition, hip-replacement surgery was out of the question.

None of it mattered, that is, except that there was no way to get Beth on her feet without help. Beth, always so kind, and generous, so ready with a laugh, was on her hands and knees in her fuzzy leopard pajamas at 2:30 in the morning, but the situation was far from comical. Beth had to admit she needed help.

Luckily, help was promptly available. Within minutes after Janet called 911, a young police officer was at the door. He was followed by three paramedics, all wearing gas masks due to the pandemic. They were kind and swift, cracking jokes to break up the tension. These men and women knew what they were doing. Without any discussion, they had Beth sit on the floor in front of the couch and got into position, one on either side of her. One stood at Beth's feet, providing resistance so her feet couldn't slide out from under her.

And 1, 2, 3, in the blink of an eye, they had her on her feet. They parried the thanks, smiling and saying, "You wouldn't believe how often we do this. All day and night."

And off they went, skilled angels back into the night.

Beth sat down in her chair. She was stunned by a new reality: she was losing her independence. The truth slammed into her gut. She was no longer the matriarch of the family, the kind overseer of all things charming and generous. Not only could she not take care of the people she loved, but she could no longer even take care of herself.

She put her head down and wept.

Chapter: Thirty

A sense of peace enveloped Beth. Like a soothing warm drink on a cold winter's night, it flowed through her body, mind, and soul. She felt weightless, buoyant.

Did I die? she wondered. *No,* she thought, when she felt her Connemara marble rosary beads in her hands. She felt the seat, the back, and the arms of her power-lift recliner around her, supporting her. *I'm still here.* She felt … different. Suffused with warmth. Cozy. At peace.

But when Beth opened her eyes, it hit her. Images of the night before. Her leg giving way underneath her. Banging into the bathroom vanity. Hitting the floor, knee first. Being unable to move. A wave of shame washed over her. She could no longer take care of herself. She was dependent on her children. A drag on them.

Beth felt nauseous. *I should have died*, she thought. *I'd rather die than live like this. I can't even take care of myself. Poor Ellery and Janet. They're shouldering the burden. Donnie's not even here. He left and he's never coming back. I'll probably never see him again.*

Beth's mental state was taking a real hit. One negative thought followed another until a toxic, hook-line-and-sinker effect occurred, pulling her under. She wanted to get up before Janet came to help her.

I can do it, Beth told herself. *I've faced difficulties before. God, I'm gonna need your help here. St. Anthony, I know you've got my back. Beth's gotta do this. I'm not gonna do that to my kids.*

Beth pressed the button on the recliner to bring her seat higher then leaned forward and gripped her walker with both hands. Putting more weight forward, she slowly, slowly pushed herself to a standing position. She made her way the short distance into the galley-style kitchen, where she struggled to lift her arm and grab a cup. A series of falls in the last two years had injured her shoulders, and she had yet to recover her mobility.

Maybe I should've listened to Janet and gone to physical therapy, she thought. She shook that off. *I can do it. I'll just pour myself a glass of milk and take my medication. No problem.*

Beth dumped the milk all over the kitchen floor.

"Oh, Beth," she muttered. "Look what you've done now."

She was standing there in her slippers in the middle of a puddle of milk when Janet waltzed into the kitchen.

"Uh, oh," said Janet. "If you wanted a milk bath, I would've drawn it for you in the tub!"

Janet slid into the chair across the table from Beth, who was still clad in fuzzy, warm pajamas. The PJs were patterned and colorful, comfortable, and easy to don and doff. Mother and daughter had just finished up their lunch—a bowl of Janet's lentil soup with carrots, onions, and toasted, whole-wheat pita.

"Well, Mama," Janet began, "maybe we should talk about what to do next."

"Ohh, noo," Beth said, smiling, "let's not." She giggled, her smile infusing her eyes and highlighting her great cheekbones, sans makeup as usual.

Janet gently persisted. "It's probably a good idea if we do. That way you can make the best choice."

Beth continued to deflect with humorous comebacks. She wasn't trying to be difficult. It just felt uncomfortable leaving one of her kids to solve her problems. She didn't want to burden any of them. But Janet continued to refocus the discussion. Faced with the reality of her early-morning dive to the bathroom tile, Beth finally agreed to look at her options.

"You could stay here and have help come in." They discussed the budget for that. It was an expensive one. When Janet brought up her and Ellery's willingness to fund that, Beth was adamant. She would not allow the "girls" to pay for her care. They probably couldn't even afford enough assistance to make it worthwhile.

The next option was for Beth to go and live with one of her children. Barbara's mental illness had unfolded in her later years. She had grown huge, dyed her hair black, and wore weird bohemian outfits she picked up at local thrift shops. Living with four dogs, one of which was half wolf, Barbara had made the entire kitchen floor into a litter box. Needless to say, not much cooking took place there. The rest of her apartment was piled with newspapers and other detritus. In short, Barbara had become a hoarder. She remained angry and still blamed her mother for everything that had gone wrong in her life. Over the years, she'd written angry letters, then angry texts that focused on how terrible she believed her life had been, and why it had all been Beth's fault. None of it was grounded in reality but living with Barbara obviously was not an option for Beth.

"Could you imagine me living with Ellery?" Beth asked.

"Well, she has the room. She has a bedroom and everything's on one floor," said Janet. "We'd just have to get you inside."

But Ellery was on her last nerve after Jason's long illness and death. In addition, the bathtub and shower were not accessible. Living with Ellery was out too.

Third option: Donnie. But then Beth would have to go to Florida.

The first obstacle there would be actually getting to Florida. While that would not be insurmountable, it *would* be excruciating. Beth's arthritis and bum right hip made moving around quite painful. Put her in a situation where she'd have to travel 1,200 miles, and that would be "quite painful" multiplied by 1,200.

Not only that, Beth added, "The heat would be terrible. Donnie and Patty don't understand how hard it is for me to get around. And all my doctors are here. I don't want to leave them."

Nor did Donnie and Patty understand that they'd have to prepare three meals a day for Beth and help her with activities of daily living. Their home presented accessibility challenges as well: getting into the house, trying to traverse the rug with her walker, then getting into and out of the shower. In short, living with Donnie was out.

That left one possibility if she was going to move in with one of her children: living with Janet and Henry. Because they had children and grandchildren in three places—Florida, New Jersey, and New

York—they spent about half the year within easy reach of all their family: partly in Florida, partly in Pennsylvania. That would mean Beth would have to travel back and forth between Florida and Pennsylvania; it would mean she'd have to leave her doctors; and it would mean accessibility issues similar to the other scenarios.

Living with Janet and Henry was out.

The final option was to move to an assisted-living facility. Luckily, Janet had the inside scoop on the state of New Jersey's homes for the elderly. Joan, an acquaintance of Janet's, had spent her career inspecting all of New Jersey's nursing homes and assisted-living facilities.

"Nursing homes are out. She's well enough for an assisted-living facility," Joan said. "I can recommend only two of them."

Janet held her breath. "Where are they?"

"The first one's in Cherry Hill."

Janet's heart sank.

"The second one's in Shrewsbury."

Woo hoo! Shrewsbury was only about 17 minutes from where Beth lived.

Joan provided Janet with all the details. When she got off the phone, Janet searched the Shrewsbury facility, Sage Terrace, through the Better Business Bureau and the Division of Consumer Affairs. When that showed up clean, she contacted the facility for openings and pricing.

Throughout this new discussion, Beth wondered, *Can I afford this? Maybe it would be better if I just died now.*

Janet contacted her cheerful real estate agent, Sally. When she arrived and did an assessment of Beth's property, she gave Beth the good news: her condo was worth more than she'd expected.

Ok, that hurdle was cleared, but Beth still needed to submit her paperwork to Sage Terrace and get a medical exam with all possible speed.

Chapter: Thirty-One

Moving day, January 8th, was cold and sunny. Beth had planned to pack little by little as the date approached, but somehow things didn't get done the way they used to. She was slow, ever so slow these days. Her hip crunched and ached; her knees cracked; her legs wept from lymphedema; and her fingers were swollen. That made it tough to move around, let alone be swift and organized.

Janet and Henry had come to the rescue. They'd shown up on January 7th with boxes, packing paper, and tape. The day, along with Beth's possessions, disappeared in a whirlwind of decisions and a flurry of activity.

Beth couldn't keep everything; she had to consolidate. Everything she looked at brought back memories. The pen-and-ink sketch of an inkwell and fountain pen that Donnie had made in middle school. The countless butterflies she'd collected, which were everywhere. Her favorite mugs, many of which had been gifts from her girls.

The only furniture she was taking was her recliner, a gift from Janet and Henry. It featured a seat that lifted her so she could stand up with a minimum of effort, a job her thighs could no longer perform.

Henry had called the township for a special pickup. Everything Beth was getting rid of went out to the curb, and the township guys came at five the next morning and cleared it away.

It was time for a fresh start.

The grandkids arrived after Janet and Henry had picked up a U-Haul truck. At six feet, four inches, David was a strapping New York City police officer. Between Henry, David, and a family friend, all Beth's belongings got loaded into the U-Haul.

Stunned, Beth looked around her. *How had it come to this? I didn't plan for things to end this way.* Her eyes stung. *I wanted to leave this place as part of my legacy for the kids and grandkids.*

Louise had brought Beth's 4-month-old great-granddaughter, Thalia Grace, to say goodbye.

"Love you, Gram," said Louise as they posed for pictures with brave smiles pasted on their faces. Louise's heart hurt as she looked around Beth's home, where they once played superheroes together.

Beth's hug was tighter than usual. "I'll see you soon."

"We'll be up to see you before you know it." Louise wiped her eyes and smiled through her tears.

Janet helped Beth out of her wheelchair and into the Toyota Highlander. Then she stowed the wheelchair in the back. They set off for Sage Terrace with Beth drinking in the sights of the place that had been her home for 36 years. Her gaze lingered on the butterfly bush next to the spot where her green garden bench had sat. She used to sit there while hummingbirds drank their fill of nectar at the feeder only inches from her face. Her neighbors used to stop by "Beth's Green Bench" and catch up on all the latest. Now the bench sat in Louise's yard. That gladdened Beth's heart. She saw the cherry tree she'd planted when the grandkids were young. Now it rose into the sky, offering shelter and shade to the birds and squirrels. Her heart was full, but she was afraid.

It was terrifying to be unable to take care of herself. Especially because she'd had to do that ever since she could remember. She'd taken care of everyone else, too. She was a nurse. She ate adversity for lunch. She never said, "Die." She gritted her teeth in the face of pain and forged ahead.

But this … this was a giant downhill snowball, gathering speed. It had rolled right over her and flattened her. It pummeled her as it gathered momentum. This was how she'd felt as a kid when her father chased her mother or Bill around the house with the nearest weapon. You never knew what would happen next, but you feared the worst. Would he hurt one of them? Would he do more than give Mom a bloody lip? Would he finally kill someone?

As David drove to his Gram's new home, his feelings in turmoil, he quickly pulled over to the side of the road. He put his head on the steering wheel and cried like the little boy he had once been.

Gram! he thought. *Not Gram!* His thoughts swirled in his mind and in his heart, eluding coherence. The march of the years had taken its toll. Gram was growing old, and she could no longer care for herself. She couldn't remain in the home where he and his sister had spent countless happy hours with her and at family gatherings. Everything had changed. David felt like someone had pulled the rug out from under him. But he was a police officer, a counterterrorism expert for the greatest city on Earth. The Big Apple. He knew better than most that life had a dirty underbelly, that dangerous circumstances could jump out at any moment and take you by surprise.

He thought back to an event just the week before, when he and his captain were driving through Harlem one evening, heading back to the station. Suddenly a large man ran toward the passenger door, hands in the air, screaming: "Help! Help! My mom's dying!"

The captain braked and David rolled down the window. He briefly questioned the man, trying to calm him down and get a coherent sentence from him so they could find out exactly what was going on. He and the captain were not on patrol in the vicinity, so technically, this wasn't his responsibility. But they were on the scene, and a woman's life might be in danger.

Of course, there was another, more sinister possibility. These were not easy times for the police. The community—the whole country, in fact, and the world in general—no longer respected the police. And with good reason. Some police were corrupt; some were renegades who played by their own rules; some were more criminal than the people they arrested. That was *some* of the police. The vast majority of the force, David knew, were people of integrity, people who wanted to help, men and women who put their lives at risk. Every. Single. Day.

There had been a slate of police ambushes in the nation, traps that angry radicals had set for the police to walk into—police officers responding to a desperate call who'd been shot on arrival. Police on break in their cruisers shot in the head. You couldn't be too careful. You wanted to go home at night. But you had a job to do. And this man could be telling the truth.

David steeled himself and followed the man into the tenement and up four flights of stairs. All the while, the man was screaming for his mama.

When David walked into the apartment, he was the only white person there. He was further set apart by his navy-blue patrol uniform. When he asked what happened, no one responded. He followed the screaming man into the bedroom, where an 80-ish woman lay unresponsive and covered in vomit.

"Did she take anything?" he looked around.

Although the crowd had followed him, no one made eye contact.

In desperation, David pleaded, "Listen, I wanna help your mom, but I need to know what's going on. If she took something, I can help, but if I give her the wrong treatment, she could die."

He looked around again. "No one's gonna get in trouble. I don't care what she took. I just want to help."

"It's heroin," came a voice from the back of the crowd.

That was all David needed. He pulled out his police-issue Narcan, pulled off the cap, stuck the needle through the rubber stopper, drew out the fluid, and injected the dose right into the woman's deltoid.

When the woman woke, he helped her into the shower so she could get cleaned up. Looking at her, he couldn't help but think of Gram. All she meant to him. And although no one thanked David for saving this woman's life, he felt a grim satisfaction at having been in the right place at the right time and overriding the potential risk to his own life. He felt good about that and hoped someone would be there for Gram in her time of need if he couldn't be.

The reality of the moment settled back on him. He wiped his eyes, pulled himself together, and got back on the road.

Chapter: Thirty-Two

Beth's four walls were closing in.

Technically, she had more than four walls. Her new home, Room 109 at Sage Terrace, was a suite with a combination bedroom, sitting area, and kitchenette. The hallway led to a bathroom equipped with a walk-in shower. Her windows in the sitting area looked out on green lawns, trees, and bushes. Birds came to the feeder in the tree outside her window and deer often grazed outside early in the morning and again at twilight.

It was a comfortable suite in a lovely place. In the public area, there was a large central kitchen that made three square meals a day. The menu offered several choices at every sitting. The coffee was a happy surprise for Beth: it was absolutely delicious.

She could shower by herself here. She hadn't done that for years. Her arthritis, muscle weakness, hip pain, and lymphedema had rendered that impossible. She had been washing up as she stood in front of the bathroom vanity inside the confines of her walker. She needed to lean with one hand on the walker as she soaped up with her other hand and a washcloth. It had been difficult, but she hadn't complained. She never did.

Janet and Henry—those two again!—had wanted to have her bathroom retrofitted to make it accessible for her, but she'd adamantly refused. Janet had called someone to come assess it anyway, but it turned out that the configuration of the tub and toilet would make it such a complicated job that it wasn't worth the extraordinary cost.

At Sage Terrace, Beth used her walker to back up against the shower chair. After she stripped, she'd sit on the chair and swing into the shower. Her right hip wasn't too happy about the movement, but it was never happy these days, and at least she could do it herself. And do it right. She was actually more independent here than she'd been at home. Now she could take her time and bask in the warm water flowing over her, scrubbing all over and getting nice and clean. That was a delicious feeling she hadn't had in years.

A nurse or an aide came in to check on her regularly. Every kind of clergyperson and medical health professional visited just as regularly. Nor would she ever go hungry here. In addition to three square meals, she could get a snack from the kitchen or a staff member whenever she wanted one. Beth had her own refrigerator and cupboards, so she had plenty of snacks and small-meal items at her fingertips. Once she could get out, she'd sit in the dining room with the other residents. There would be socialization opportunities at meals and during activities. A Catholic priest would come on Friday to say the rosary and on Sunday to say Mass although that would have to be outside during this stage of Covid-19. There was bingo, too, and movie night.

But Beth was adrift. She felt so unconnected to this place. All of her belongings, placed in their new spots, were out of order. She didn't know where anything was. It wasn't her home.

Since the country—really, the world—was still struggling with the pandemic, Beth was confined to her room for two whole weeks. Fourteen days during which she'd have to stay *in her room*. She was overcome by a tidal wave of grief. She wept over the injustice, the pain of it all.

She had several conversations with Our Lord over the situation. Why had she had to leave her home, her little condo? She didn't want much. She just wanted to stay there. But now it was on the market, and they were having an open house tomorrow. Real Estate Sally thought the condo would sell quickly.

She didn't want it to sell. She wanted to go back. She wanted to get her own meals whenever she wanted them. She wanted to take her walker to the front door at 10 minutes to 10 in the morning and meet Jeff, the man who dropped off her Meals on Wheels during the week. They would exchange a word or two. She wanted to say good morning to Garrett, the mailman. She'd known him for decades and had "watched" his twins grow up, had commiserated with him on the troubles that befell the post office, had prayed for him when he went into the hospital for a heart transplant. She wanted to plant her own flowers in her own yard and put out her own bird feeders.

Beth stopped. She could no longer bend down to plant flowers or pull weeds. Even if she were willing to try, it wouldn't be safe. She'd likely fall over—*if* she could get over the threshold and down the step from the doorway to the cement pad that ran along the front of her flower beds. She had to admit to herself that she could no longer manage even that. She was now a "shut-in."

The realization knocked her back mentally and emotionally. She pictured herself like a full, white garbage bag—tied up, secured, and set out at the curb. Dirty and worthless.

Beth gazed around her room, shadowed in the January light. The walls appeared impenetrable, and there might as well be no door at all. She couldn't leave this room. Her heart shriveled up, and, as she sat in her easy chair, she wept bitter tears.

Chapter: Thirty-Three

When day 15 arrived, Beth was sprung from her apartment. She could go to the dining room for meals and was free to move about as she pleased.

The last two weeks had been a test. Beth had had her ups and downs—mostly downs. She'd wept, not slept, and prayed. Prayed for peace, prayed for relief. Prayed for clarity. Prayed for forgiveness. Prayed for a change of heart. She'd given her Connemara marble rosary beads a good polishing.

She'd gotten darn tired of praying even if she did have a special devotion to Our Lady and St. Anthony. Eventually, she said to herself, "Okay, Beth, ya gotta go along with it or you're gonna sink."

Once she made that determination, she didn't waver from it. She had a lot of company—more than she wanted, really. Okay, she didn't see Jeff the Meals on Wheels guy, but here there were Consuelo and

Jimmy, who cooked and served her meals. She no longer saw Garrett the mailman, but now she had Ian the chiropractor—imagine that! —who came to adjust her. That was a real treat, a service that she'd never have sought out for herself. It made her back feel so much better. She also had a male physician's assistant who came to see her once a month. He was Irish, had a great sense of humor, and told funny stories. The podiatrist came to treat her feet. Beth had always thought her feet were ugly—thanks, Mom, for making fun of my "big" feet in front of your friends—but the podiatrist was taking great care of them, and they were looking good.

The Monday after Beth had moved in, a nurse had come to her room and administered the Pfizer vaccine against SARS-CoV-2. Beth and the other residents were among the first in the United States to receive the vaccine, and Beth felt very lucky. Even better, she felt blessed. Her life wasn't over. She had plenty of life left to live and to appreciate all her blessings.

She also wanted to continue her life's purpose, which was to lay down her life for her family. Being here, being safe, having great medical care, an abundance of healthy food, and people to see and with whom to talk made things better for Beth and better for her family, too.

Chapter: Thirty-Four

Beth had her "aha" moment after she'd been released from quarantine in mid-January. It could have been a brutal time of scarcity. Snow kept falling, seemingly isolating her and the other residents inside the building. The air outside was bitter cold. Beth saw the creatures outside her window struggling to survive.

She both identified with them and differentiated herself from them. She'd been forced by life to be isolated from her family and her former life, from the creature comforts and familiarity of her home of 36 years. Some might say the landscape of her life was bitter cold.

Yet Beth had so much. That's how she chose to look at it. It was a choice, she told herself. Abe Lincoln had said that a man is as happy as he made up his mind to be. She figured Abe wouldn't mind if she interpreted the proverb to include her gender.

And look at Abe! she thought. He was a man of many sorrows, just like Christ. Born dirt-poor in a log cabin, Lincoln was self-educated. He lost jobs, was defeated over and over in his quest for public office. He failed in business and suffered the loss of his sweetheart. He had a nervous breakdown, for heaven's sake! His beloved son, Willie, died at age 11, and his wife was mentally unbalanced. Despite his personal anguish, Abe retained his sense of humor, his fortitude, and often spoke so eloquently that his proverbs and sayings remain popular today. Beth would follow that maxim and be as happy as she could be.

She walked quite slowly in her walker, but she could get around by herself. It was good exercise for her, the physical therapist said. Of course, Beth knew that herself. As a nurse, she'd encouraged countless patients to get up and walk around, understanding that movement would help restore their health. Beth knew that once she got into a wheelchair, she'd never get out of it. She was staying upright and mobile as long as her body allowed her to do so. She'd fight the good fight. Along the way, she encouraged everyone she met.

One of those people was Shirley. Shirley was 94 years old. She and her husband, Franklin, who was 96, had moved into Sage Terrace together. Franklin hadn't lasted long. After his death, Shirley simply shut down. She'd been the quiet one in the relationship, and Franklin had balanced out the duo with his outgoing, affable nature. Once he died, Shirley was out of kilter.

The staff encouraged Shirley to come out to meals, and she did, but she'd sit there staring at her plate as if she were in a catatonic state.

Beth had to pass Shirley's table for every meal. "Good morning, Shirley," Beth would say. "It's good to see you this morning. What's for breakfast?" At first, Shirley would ignore her. After a while, though, Shirley began to respond. "Good morning," she'd whisper.

As the days and weeks went by, Shirley began to look up as Beth came by. Beth was pleased to see her progress. One morning when Beth greeted her, Shirley looked up and met Beth's gaze. Suddenly, a smile broke out on her face. It was like the sun coming out from behind a cloud, and Beth could feel her own heart open.

As Beth continued to make her way into the dining room, she had to pass Steve's table. That's where "the guys" sat, six men who'd all served in the military and seen action on their respective battlefields. Beth loved to hear their stories, even if Steve did tease her about being so slow.

"C'mon, Beth, move it!" he'd cajole. "What's taking you so long?"

She'd give it right back to him. "Hey, at least I'm upright. I'd like to see you try to move when you're my age, especially if you had this hip."

Steve was quite young for an assisted-living facility, in his early 70s. He seemed to be in good mental and physical health, but people often had maladies and challenges that were easy to conceal.

One day, Steve surprised her with a horn she could attach to her walker. "You can beep it to warn us that you're coming."

It was a standing joke, and Beth used her knee to sound the horn as she rounded the corner for every meal.

While some people teased Beth about her slow walking, Alfred Li envied her. A small, withered man in a wheelchair, Alfred resembled a praying mantis with horn-rimmed glasses. When Beth stopped at his table to say hello, he wiped his mouth with a cloth napkin and said, "Oh, Beth, I'd give anything to be able to walk like you." Beth patted his shoulder. "You're doing fine, Alfred."

Beth's table was smaller than Steve's and seated four women: Ellen, Dawn, and Francine were her dining companions at every meal. They bonded quickly. Ellen was a cultured woman who'd also been a nurse. She was attractive, with mocha-colored skin, wavy chestnut hair, and a full, ready smile. Ellen's mild dementia revealed itself during dinner one evening when she informed her dining companions that she'd arrived at Sage Terrace in a rickshaw after her children had auctioned off her home and possessions.

Beth knew from previous conversations that Ellen had sold her home after her husband passed away and had moved in with her daughter and her son-in-law. Trusting her nursing training and experience that it was a good idea to keep others grounded in reality, Beth said, "Ellen, you said that you lived with your daughter after you sold your home. Isn't that right?"

Ellen didn't have a good answer and flubbed her way through it. From time to time, she would tell the same story of her rickshaw arrival and of her children's conspiracy to defraud her. Nevertheless, she remained an otherwise charming dinner companion.

Dawn was an Elvis Presley lover and kept a life-size cardboard Elvis in her room. With alabaster skin and circles of red rouge, Dawn looked slightly clown-like. She was a bit foggy but overall was pleasant and easy to please.

Francine had been a teacher and had six children. She'd grown up in the most affluent area in Leymouth County, in a manor house on the water. She and her husband purchased her childhood home as newlyweds, and she'd lived there all her life. After her husband's death, the huge house became too much for her, so she sought refuge at Sage Terrace. As a resident, everything would be taken care of for her. She and Beth often had stimulating conversations at their meals. It was one of the many benefits of living in an "old-age home."

Of course, not all the residents were pleasant or mild-mannered. Seth, the man in the next room, talked to himself day and night. Sometimes he was angry and had terrible, foul-mouthed arguments with unseen adversaries. Other times, he'd wail as if he were a little boy having a nightmare. Unfortunately, that usually took place in the middle of the night, making it hard for Beth to sleep.

Then there was Rocco. Rocco was short, stocky, and spoke with a heavy Italian accent. His parents were Sicilian, and English was his second language. His threatening demeanor made comparing him to the Mafia pretty realistic.

For some reason, Rocco had taken an immediate dislike to Beth. He was rude, aggressive, and physically threatening, often invading her body space. But even though she was physically vulnerable, Beth didn't back down. She hadn't raised four children and nursed all kinds of people without learning some techniques for handling people like him.

Scowling at her, Rocco leaned in so close that Beth could smell his garlic breath. “You go!” he shouted at her. “Go back to your room!”

Astonished and rattled, Beth steeled herself and didn’t flinch. “What’s gotten under your skin today, Rocco?” she asked in a mild tone of voice. She went about her business, ignoring him as if he were a mere shadow.

After several of these types of incidents, Rocco mellowed. He even became conciliatory toward Beth, treating her with his rough version of gallantry.

Score another one for Beth! Winner takes all. But Beth didn’t gloat. She just wanted to get along. To go along and not sink. To lay down her life for her friends and her family. But that was before Sylvia.

Sylvia had replaced Francine, who, sadly, had passed on. Unlike the affable Francine, Sylvia was haughty and rude. Despite all her affluence and braggadocio, Sylvia seemed envious of Beth. At every meal, Sylvia had something cutting to say. She had a tongue like a viper.

“Oh, Beth,” she’d sneer, “why are you so slow?” or “Just didn’t feel like getting dressed up today, darling?” and she’d roll her eyes at Dawn and Ellen.

Wounded at first, Beth understood that Sylvia was an unhappy person. But that didn’t make meals any more pleasant. Meals became even more of a trial when Ellen began to behave like Sylvia, and Beth's friendship and happy conversations with her ended. Beth was surprised and hurt that Ellen had followed Sylvia's lead.

Beth struggled with her feelings over this new, unpleasant development. She didn't talk about it to anyone, but Janet ferreted it out during a phone conversation. Once Janet turned on her cross-examination skills, you might as well tell all. She'd get it out of you regardless. If you fessed up early, the torture didn't last as long.

"Why don't you request to be moved to a different table?" Janet had suggested. She was exasperated that Beth's new table companion, a woman in her eighties, was behaving like a mean high school girl. She probably *had* been a mean girl in high school. Some things never change.

"Well, I'll just wait and see what happens." That was a standard Beth reply.

"We know what's gonna happen," Janet continued. "Sylvia will continue to be mean and snarky and ruin all your meals."

That's exactly what happened. But other residents had taken notice. None of them liked it.

Beth was well-liked by this time. She had a kind word for everyone. She was funny and told good stories. People had met her children, grandchildren, great-grandchildren, and even a great-granddog who had visited. Bentley—Ben-Ben for short—was a very well-behaved black Labrador. He came to visit Gram from time to time with David, his wife, Sarah, and their two baby girls. Louise and Thalia Grace came often. The residents liked Beth's family. Various family members would walk Beth to lunch or dinner during the visits and stop at all the tables with Beth to say hello and exchange a few pleasantries. They would dress in their best for their visits. The older folks liked that; it showed respect.

Sylvia's envy simmered under the surface. Until the day.

Chapter: Thirty-Five

The low buzz of morning conversation provided a backdrop to the clink of silverware against the everyday china as Beth navigated her walker toward the dining room. As she neared her table, Richard jumped up and pulled out her chair for her.

Eying this sweet display of good manners, Sylvia was unable to contain her toxic jealousy. Narrowing her eyes, she sneered, "Oh, look! It's everybody's darling."

In the seat next to Sylvia, even Ellen had to bite her tongue to keep from crying out, "What a bitch!"

Beth smiled. It wasn't that nasty barbs from jealous, sour women didn't hurt. It was that Beth refused to engage in that kind of negativity, refused to be brought to that woman's level.

The rest of the residents had no such compunctions. Richard, who sat at the next table, stood back up. "You know what, Sylvia? You're right. Beth *is* everybody's darling!" Then Richard turned to the room, raised his glass, and called out: "Here's to Beth! Everybody's darling!"

"Hear, hear!" everyone cheered. After all, the place was filled with people who'd been touched by Beth's kindness and generosity. From employees and residents alike, cries of "To Beth!" filled the dining hall. "To Beth!"

Humiliated and feeling an unknown emotion—shame—Sylvia slunk out of the room, slithering along in her own muck like a slug in the darkness.

Beth ducked her head in embarrassment. She truly did not want anyone's feelings to be hurt, nor did she wish to be championed. She also felt shame. *Is Sylvia right?* she wondered. *Should I dress better? Am I really worthless?*

Her mind raced through her life and everything she'd lost as if she were watching a movie: Her parents' love. Her sister, Prissy. Her husbands. Her ability to drive her car. The car itself. Her ability to walk independently. Her home. Her ability to live independently. Her choice about when to eat a meal. Her ability to give money and gifts to others. Her dinner companions. Even the dinner companion who'd turned on her.

Beth had expected to feel hollowed out, sad, empty. It had all come to this, to being closeted in a home with only elderly residents, some of whom gossiped and backbit as if they were still in high school. To having dinner with Sylvia, who hated her for no good reason.

But as she reviewed each loss in her mind, Beth felt a sense of freedom. Of companionship. She wasn't alone. She had her family, which was growing all the time. Babies, babies, everywhere! Her children, her grandchildren, her great-grandchildren—even Ben-Ben—came to visit. In the meantime, she didn't have to worry about where her next meal was coming from. She had built-in company, including the staff, who also responded to Beth's nurturing and her interest in them and their loved ones. She had her own spot in the big home where she could go for a bit of peace and quiet. There, she could shower when she wanted, she could nap, read, watch the news or a Hallmark movie, and she could look out on the beautiful bounties of nature, including the wild creatures who lived just beyond her window.

She was 91 years old, for heaven's sake! She could let go of what others thought of her and of the people-pleasing she'd done since the days of walking on eggshells around a drunken father, a pitiless stepmother, a mother who would smack her for no reason, a husband who thought so little of his marriage vows that he'd laugh about giving her a venereal disease. Her mind rolled over the years, over all of the love she had received from friends, from family. She realized that she *had* lain down her life for her friends and family, that giving and receiving love had fulfilled her, had given her layer upon layer of worth.

She thought of something Janet—her daughter, the lawyer—had said. In a legal case, the lawyer must build a wall of evidence. Lawyers do it brick by brick. Each brick is another piece of evidence. Conversely—*a good legal word*, Beth chuckled to herself—your own worth is intrinsic but is also built brick by brick, with every act of love and kindness you do. And everyone did love her. They told her often enough. She realized they really meant it. She felt a shift inside her, like planets re-aligning. Like trajectories gliding into place. Like stars shooting in all directions and leaving gold stardust in their wakes. Beth had it all; she knew that now. She felt whole. She *was* whole. And for the first time in her life, she felt worthwhile.

How funny is that? she thought to herself. *Wouldn't Sylvia hate that? I really am everybody's darling.*

Acknowledgments

While this novel is a work of fiction, some of it is based upon my mother's life experience. I wanted to create a work that showcases the quiet strength and courage she has demonstrated throughout her entire life. The older I get, the more I realize just how extraordinary she really is. Thank you, Mom, for putting up with me and my ideas.

I am grateful to my writing group for all their support and camaraderie, especially Dr. Richard Nongard, Tamelynda Lux, Dr. Linda (Bk) Wells, James M. Vera, and Rusty Williams.

Thank you to my editor, Vincent Czyz, for his meticulous work.

Thank you to my ever-present cheering squad: my daughter, Theresa Sullivan; my son and his wife, Kevin and Sarah Sullivan; and my son and his wife, Curt and Diara Wesler.

Finally, I am very grateful to my husband and best friend, Richard Wesler, for his constancy and good nature, as well as his proofreading skills.

9 798986 412412